A Father's Gift

Book Two—San Antonio Series

Endorsements

Paula Peckham brings a refreshing voice to Christian fiction. *A Father's Gift* is a charming story of discovery for a young man facing fatherhood for the first time. There is never a dull moment as Manny Blair revisits the past, entertains strangers, and digs up secrets to learn how to navigate his and his family's future. Paula reminds us the journey to self-discovery is never easy, nor does it often come at a convenient time, but it is so worth it.
—Joy K. Massenburge, author of *A Heart Surrendered*.

Paula Peckham's created a relatable cast of characters in this sweet romantic Christmas novella. It's the perfect holiday read.
—Karin Beery, author of Hopeful Fiction with a Healthy Dose of Romance.

A Father's Gift

Book Two—San Antonio Series

Paula Peckham

Copyright Notice

A Father's Gift Book Two—San Antonio Series

First edition. Copyright © 2022 by Paula Peckham. The information contained in this book is the intellectual property of Paula Peckham and is governed by United States and International copyright laws. All rights reserved. No part of this publication, either text or image, may be used for any purpose other than personal use. Therefore, reproduction, modification, storage in a retrieval system, or retransmission, in any form or by any means, electronic, mechanical, or otherwise, for reasons other than personal use, except for brief quotations for reviews or articles and promotions, is strictly prohibited without prior written permission by the publisher.

This is a work of fiction. Names, characters, businesses, places, events, locales, and incidents are either the products of the author's imagination or used in a fictitious manner. Any resemblance to actual persons, living or dead, or actual events is purely coincidental.

Cover and Interior Design:
Editor(s): Cristel Phelps, Deb Haggerty

PUBLISHED BY: Elk Lake Publishing, Inc., 35 Dogwood Drive, Plymouth, MA 02360, 2022

Library Cataloging Data

Names: Peckham, Paula (Paula Peckham)

A Father's Gift Book Two—San Antonio Series/ Paula Peckham

140 p. 23cm × 15cm (9in × 6 in.)

ISBN-13: 978-1-64949-682-9 (paperback) | 978-1-64949-683-6 (trade hardcover) | 978-1-64949-684-3 (trade paperback) | 978-1-64949-685-0

Key Words: Western, romance, abandonment, pregnancy, childbirth, murder, Christian novel

Library of Congress Control Number: 2022945433

Dedication

This book is dedicated to the long line of capable, independent women in my life who taught me to be strong and shared with me the love of reading. What perfect gifts you've shared. I love you.

Chapter One

SAN ANTONIO, TEXAS, 1863

"Let's go, boys. Time to head home." Manny climbed onto the seat and slapped the reins against the backs of his long-suffering oxen. The wagon groaned, wheels pressing deep ruts into the ground. He glanced behind him.

Maybe I got carried away.

He'd cut down some small trees where the creek ran parallel to the road in front of his property. He loaded the last of the cut wood, wiping sweat from his brow despite the chill in the early December air. His list of chores before the baby came just decreased by one. They would have plenty of fuel for warmth or cooking once his son arrived.

Enough wood to last two winters filled the bed of the wagon. He shrugged. Being prepared was a good thing.

Excitement and unease competed in his chest, the same as he'd felt when Dr. Simpson confirmed Abby's hunch. Her pregnancy was a dream come true. But this dream dragged thunderclouds behind it. Manny swallowed the discomfort that sprang to mind every time he thought of the impending birth. He had little experience with fatherhood, none with babies.

His dad had disappeared. At the age of five, Manny didn't understand why it had happened. He only knew his father never came home. Card games were more important to Mark Blair than his family. That wouldn't happen with his son. He'd be there.

Stories that spoke of generational curses filled the Bible. Sons who were punished for the sins of their fathers.

What if I'm a sorry father too? What if he let his child down? All four of the baby's grandparents—his and Abby's folks—were with Jesus now. If he didn't pass muster, it would fall to sweet Yaideli to step in. She'd have to give up the worry-free job of great-grandmother and take on the mantle of a dad. Again.

He clenched his jaw. That wouldn't happen. No matter what the cost.

The oxen strained against the load he'd given them. An ominous creak sounded from underneath. Manny ignored the warning sound from the wagon. His worry took precedence.

Are my expectations for myself unrealistic? The sins of the father ...

"No. I declare here and now that Abby and Manny Blair will be good parents. We'll be *great* parents. Whatever little soul God has sent is safe with us. We'll provide everything baby Blair needs."

He climbed down and moved to the head of the oxen. He could walk instead of ride. Ease the load a bit. "Come on, boys. Put your backs into it." He patted an encouraging hand on the withers of the nearest animal.

Crack.

Manny crouched and peered under the heavily loaded bed. A slat bent down in the shape of a splintered V. A muffled curse escaped before he could stop it, and impatience curdled his stomach. Biting back words of complaint, he walked to the tailgate and pulled the first log off. At least half of the load would have to come out of the wagon.

A Father's Gift

"Hey there, friend. Seems like you could use a hand." A kind voice called from the road.

Manny turned to find an older gentleman standing at the road, looking on with a tentative smile. The man had a long, lanky body and stood stoop-shouldered. Deep lines grooved his face. He seemed a little worse for wear, his clothes dirty and threadbare. Manny squinted. No one he knew.

He gave the stranger a nod. "Actually, I could use some help. I don't like being away from the house too long. My wife is *en cinta*, and ... well, I worry about her a little. I wanted to be back by now."

"The devil finds work for idle hands." The old man spread his own empty ones wide. "I'd be happy to help you unload, if that's what you're doing."

Manny eyed him with a dubious glance. Weariness screamed from the other man's thin body. But picking up one log at a time and stacking it on the ground wouldn't be too hard.

"Sure, I'd be grateful. Name's Manny." He walked over to the road, pulled off a glove, and extended his hand.

The man reached out and gripped it, dipping his chin in greeting. "Gabe. Proud to know you."

The two men returned to the wagon and attacked the heaping pile of cut wood with a rhythmic gusto.

Gabe paused to catch his breath. He nodded toward Manny. "Looks like you had a run-in with a fire at some point in your past."

Manny huffed a surprised laugh, touching his face with his fingertips. "Yeah. I did. It's funny. There was a time in my life these scars were the only thing on my mind when I ran into someone in town, met a new person. Since Abby came into my life, I hardly think of them at all. She doesn't seem to notice them, so I forget they're there."

"What happened, if you don't mind my asking?" Gabe leaned against the wagon, a curious look on his face.

"Sleeping in the barn with my cousins at a wedding. Hay caught fire. Got out alive by the skin of my teeth."

Gabe tsked. "What a shame for a tragedy like that to happen on a day of joy. Must've had a guardian angel on your shoulder."

"Something like that." Manny agreed.

He turned back to the wood. Soon, the stack on the ground was almost equal to the amount in the wagon. Manny clapped the man on the back with a grateful hand. "Do you live in San Antonio? I don't recall seeing you before."

"Just passin' through." Gabe answered in a diffident manner. "Don't really have a destination in mind. Followin' the prompting of the Holy Spirit."

"Well, I'm glad the Spirit sent you my way. If you're going to be around for a bit, I may have some chores for hire. I'd be pleased to work with you again."

The man flattened his palm against his chest as he gave a slight bow. "Thank you, friend. I believe I'll be in town for a while. Have some old business to take care of. You can find me there."

"Maybe we'll see each other. You have somewhere to stay the night?"

Gabe shrugged. "I'm sure I'll find a place. God provides."

Nodding, Manny shook his hand again. "That he does. I need to get home now. Thanks, again."

He climbed back on the wagon and slapped the reins. His thoughts moved to the woman waiting for him. "I'm coming, Abby. Be well until I can get there."

After limping the buckboard home, he stopped the oxen near the barn and glanced around. As he unhitched them,

Abby's horse walked up to the fence with a welcoming nicker.

"Hey, Bird. Where's our little mama?" The horse tipped her ears toward him. He patted the long nose sticking over the top rail. "Did she go see Yaideli without you?"

The sound of retching drew his worried gaze. *Not again. This isn't normal, is it, God?* He turned to search for his wife. There. At the garden.

Abby kneeled in the wheat-colored Texas prairie grass, curled over like a wooly worm preparing for the coming winter.

Fear coiled in Manny's belly. His mother had died only days after he was born. History could *not* repeat itself. The concept of life without Abby was unthinkable. His utter inability to help her, to make things better for her, brought him to his knees every night. *God, please protect her. I want this baby, but I want Abby more. Please ...*

He jogged to Abby's side and crouched beside her. "What can I do to help?"

Wisps of hair escaped from her braid. He stroked them away from her wan, tired face. Worry filled him again. He pulled her close, wrapping his arms around the protruding middle, tucking her head beneath his chin. A sudden flash of resentment flooded his chest. Resentment toward his unborn child.

Appalled, he stomped the thought. "No, no, no."

Maybe his father had felt the same toward him after his mother died when he was four days old. Is that why he dad chose to drink and gamble instead of spending time with him? Until it killed him?

Abby patted his chest. "I'm OK, Manny. It's not as bad today as some days. I'll be all right."

He pasted a smile on his face. "Wouldn't you be more comfortable resting on the bed instead of the grass?" His sarcasm could almost always make her laugh.

"I didn't plan on plopping down when I walked out here." Abby shot an arch look at him as she straightened in his arms.

Ah, good. There's that spunk. "Are you done tossing your breakfast?" *Please smile. Feel happy.*

She pushed herself from the ground to a crouch. "Not sure I'll be much good to anyone today, but I think I'm OK." She stilled, her attention transferring to the child inside.

He sighed with resignation when her concentration switched focus. The past few months had made an uncomfortable new reality quite clear. The baby had bumped Manny to second string in the household.

"Are you done, little one? No more complaints for now?" Abby paused, as if hearing a reply in her mind.

Manny placed a hand under her elbow as she struggled to her feet with a grunt. The changes brought on by pregnancy had grown progressively obvious, and her balance was questionable these days. She straightened, placing her fists against the small of her back, then stretched, groaning against the discomfort.

Sham, the shaggy white dog who'd appeared at the farm last year and adopted them as his family, waited at her feet. Abby leaned down and patted his head. "Thanks for sitting with me, boy. It takes a while for me to get things done these days, doesn't it? You're such a patient friend."

Manny stroked Abby's belly with a gentle touch, spoke to the mound. "I hope this isn't a portent of things to come, Little Man. You've been pretty bossy all this time. Go ahead and get it all out of your system now."

Abby chuckled, a thin sound. "The doctor said I'll feel fine once the baby gets here. If for no other reason, I'm hoping our *daughter* comes quickly."

Once on her feet, a wave of weakness made Abby pause.

What if the baby's coming-out part is as hard as the getting-here part has been?

Worry held her captive in the darkness of night. Women died from childbirth all the time. Manny's own mother had. There were no guarantees for a successful delivery.

What if mine is a bad one? What if ...

Often, while lying sleepless next to Manny, she talked with her mother in her mind. *Mama, send me your wisdom in a dream. If ever I needed you, now's the time.*

On those occasions, she would blink back tears of grief and fear. Emotions rode close to the surface these days. Missing her mom at her wedding had been bad, but it was nothing compared to this. As the weeks counted down, Abby's nerves wound up, tighter and tighter.

Working in the garden was easier now that the heat from summer had dissipated. And making baby clothes under Yaideli's watchful eye, sitting in front of the fireplace at her grandmother-in-law's cozy, cheerful house relaxed her. Yaideli was gratifyingly interested in the coming birth of her great-grandchild. *Thank you, God, for her.* She counted her lucky stars the older woman would be there for her. If she couldn't have her mother, her grandmother-in-love was the next-best thing.

Now, however, here in the weak winter sunshine, she sucked in a breath of resolution and smiled at Manny. "Remember what Dr. Simpson when we saw him? He told us to go home and enjoy the baby growing inside." The old man had patted her hand kindly. "I don't think he realized I'd still be feeling this puny seven-and-a-half months in."

"His exact words were 'worry will stunt the baby'."

Manny stroked her face with curled knuckles. "Follow his advice and try to think happy thoughts."

Easy for him to say.

"I have happy thoughts." Abby remonstrated, her voice defensive. "I'm happy she's coming. I want her, and I'm looking forward to meeting her. But I can't help thinking of all the things that could go wrong." She paused, swallowed. "I don't want her to take it personally."

She stroked her hand across her swollen abdomen. "Could you stop whatever you're doing to cause this, please, Baby Girl? I'm mighty tired of ginger tea and toast." *And feeling weak and tired all the time.* "Come on. Let's go back to the house." Abby clasped Manny's hand in hers, lifting her cheek for his kiss.

At her feet, Sham's tail swept across the grass, tongue lolling while he watched her. She smiled at him, taking comfort in his presence. When they turned to go, she spied the wagon, groaning under its load. She stared. Cocking an eyebrow in amazement, she looked at Manny. "Are there any trees left near the creek?"

He blushed when he bent to retrieve the basket she'd carried to the garden, the bottom covered with the scrawny harvest of the last of the gourds—squash, a small pumpkin, a single cantaloupe. He propped it on his hip. "Laugh if you want. You'll be glad of it when February gets here, bringing sleet and ice." He paused, then ducked his head. "The other half is still sitting on the ground. I broke the wagon."

Abby laughed. The smile fled her face as nausea roiled inside her again. "No." She groaned and bent at the waist.

Nature took over. Her words spilled onto the ground, along with the remnants of her scant breakfast. Sham whined, his tongue taking a comforting swipe at the hand she had braced on her knee.

Fear settled in.

What if I die?

Abby lay on the bed while Sham curled in front of the fire. A weak smile tipped the corners of her mouth. She stifled her sigh at the smell of the steeping ginger Manny prepared in the kitchen.

She fought to overcome her grouchiness, struggling to a sitting position, plumping a pillow behind her back. "God, help me to feel grateful. Give me the right spirit." She stroked her distended abdomen while murmuring the prayer.

As if adding her own voice to the conversation, the baby surged inside, causing a swell to roll from one side of her belly to the other. Abby chuckled, placing her hand on top of the undulation with a gentle touch. "Yes, Baby Girl, I hear you. I'm sorry I grumble about you. I wish we could co-exist more peacefully."

A sharp jab produced a lump in her side. Wrinkling her nose, she pressed back, nudging the offending knee or elbow back toward her center. "Hey, now. Behave yourself, little rascal. That's my body you're stretching from here to Kingdom come." Love softened her scold, for despite the misery the past few months had brought, Abby wanted this child like the earth wanted the sunrise each day.

Manny appeared in the doorway, mug cradled in his hand. "Talking to yourself?" He smiled.

She stretched out a welcoming arm. "Come feel. She's doing her daily exercises."

He sat on the edge of the bed. Abby guided his hand

to where the babe kicked. He gasped, then laughed softly. "He's a strong 'un, that's for sure."

They shared a conspiratorial glance, neither willing to concede to the other's surety about the gender of their unborn child.

Finally, the baby stilled. Abby nudged Manny. "Out of my way. I've got laundry waiting."

He remained where he was. "Give it a few more minutes." He pressed the mug into her hands. "Drink this. Then let the tea settle."

She frowned, but leaned back with a disgruntled sigh. Sipping from the mug, she hid her grimace, then handed it back to him. "I'm fine."

"Ten more minutes."

Abby pressed her lips together, impatience settling under her breastbone like heartburn. This was silly. There was so much to do.

Her eyelids fluttered. *OK. Ten minutes.*

Abby's eyes opened. She looked around, aghast. "How long was I asleep?" She called through the doorway to Manny, standing in the kitchen.

"As long as you needed to be."

Love swelled her heart as she watched from her cozy position on the bed while Manny washed the dishes. His black hair was pulled back into a ponytail that reached down between his shoulder blades. A memory of that hair draping in a silky curtain around her face in the flickering light from the fire as he moved over her made her sigh. The sight of him warmed her.

That part of their marriage was on hold. The absence

of the nights of passion they'd shared for the past several months caused an ache inside. The pressure of the growing babe made intimacy uncomfortable. She longed for those moments of bliss with him.

He's seen me at my worst these past seven months. He's never going to feel attracted to me again.

Dusty pants encased his long legs. Boots caked with mud from the banks of the creek sat on the floor by the door. A big toe protruded through the knitted yarn of his sock. She'd carry that to Yaideli's to be fixed the next time she went. He reached across the cabinet to set a dried plate down. She saw him in profile. His body was lean, stomach flat. He turned back to the sink. She admired the breadth of his shoulders. Her husband was a gorgeous man, and she loved him.

He worked from sunup to sundown these days. He had the normal chores to do on the farm, plus the list he'd added on to prepare for the baby. And now he was doing her work as well. She rolled to her side and curled, folding her hands beneath her head.

All the still-remaining work for the day loomed over her like the thunder following a lightning bolt. It was coming, inescapable. She yawned, pushed herself up from the bed.

Manny turned.

"Stay in bed, Abby-girl. Yaideli is bringing supper over when she returns with the laundry. You relax."

Yaideli had come and gone?

He smiled at her, drying a plate with a dishtowel. "How do you feel? Want something to eat?"

She paused, focusing her energies internally. No waves crashed. No nausea lurked. Her stomach growled. Relief washed over her. "Yes. For once, I want something to eat."

Chapter Two

Manny spent much of his time that fall celebrating and planning. Or worrying. Some days, all three. After years of running the farm he inherited from his dad, he could do most of the chores with half a brain. Thoughts of the coming baby consumed the other half. And if he was honest with himself, the worrying part took center stage.

They had driven the wagon into San Antonio to visit the doctor in June, after a week of Abby waking up sick in the mornings.

"Congratulations. You're gonna have a baby. I speculate somewhere around the latter half of January."

At the doctor's words, a dizzying combination of nerves and elation surged through Manny, leaving him trembling.

"Er, what should we expect? I mean, while she's … expecting. And, um, after." Manny's ears had burned when he forced the questions out. As an only child, he had no experience with babies.

He hated admitting his deficiency in knowledge. With no man around to consult, no memories to mine, Manny was clueless and quite certain he would make a total mess of it all. *Blood is thicker than water. What if I'm just like him? No good?*

The kind old doctor merely thumped Manny on the back. "She'll do fine. Why don't you leave worrying about all that stuff to the little lady? I imagine she knows what's coming. You just have the cigars ready to hand out. The midwife will take care of the rest."

The conversation with the doc left Manny even more insecure about bringing his questions up. Surely, other men concerned themselves with the process. How could they not?

Then he stumbled onto a treasure trove of expertise. He volunteered to help his neighbor Hank add a room to his home. Apparently, Hank's wife was expecting a child as well. One afternoon while he was at their house, standing near an open window, he overheard a conversation and discovered women talked about babies. A lot.

About carrying them. About birthing them. About raising them.

From that day forward, Manny lurked in doorways and loitered outside the open windows when he came to help build the room. His ears perked when he heard the word "baby."

He shared his fascinating new knowledge with his friend, Jonathan, each day before heading home to Abby.

"Did you know her ... her"—he held his hands in front of his chest like he was cupping cantaloupes—"will swell?" Manny darted a furtive glance around Jonathan's barn, checking for eavesdroppers now that he knew it was so easy to do.

Jonathan, ever the supportive friend, raised a blond eyebrow, acknowledging that bonus with a pleased smile. "Well, that should be fun."

Manny scowled. "Not swelling for me, idiot. Preparing to make milk. For the baby."

Jonathan shrugged, obviously unfazed by Manny's indignation. "It can still be fun."

Heat flushed Manny's face. He plowed on. "But they'll get tender. Sore to the touch." He refused to be talked out of his nerves by the teasing.

Jonathan yielded. "OK. Not so fun for her, then."

Manny pictured Abby and the mornings spent heaving into a bowl placed on the floor by the bed. "I don't think *any* of this has been fun for her."

Manny met Jonathan in his front field to help sort the bull calves. He brought up his new knowledge again. "The ladies at Hank's house said morning sickness is supposed to go away after the first three months or so. Abby still throws up. Quite often. Sometimes more than once a day. She's getting thinner, not fatter. I'm worried."

Jonathan pointed a finger. "This is all your fault, you know. She probably hates you by now." He chuckled.

Manny was silent.

Jonathan frowned. "I was kidding. She doesn't hate you."

"I'd hate me if I was her."

"Be reasonable. It took both of you to get to this point. How could either of you know she'd have a harder time than normal with morning sickness?"

Manny didn't respond.

"You're quite the wet blanket these days, my friend."

Jonathan's mutter was ignored.

The day after the job was finished, the friends went hunting. Manny said, "You're never gonna believe this one." He stared at Jonathan with horror congealing in his gut. He still couldn't credit what he'd overheard. "Martha told Juanita her daughter, Jessie, had her bloody show."

Jonathan drew back, his lip curling. "What's *that*?" He squinted. "And who's Martha? And Juanita?"

"Martha, the lady at church whose husband died of a heart attack last year. And Juanita who has a food stand in the square with the Chili Queens. As for what it is, I have no clue. But from what I gather, it happens very near the end."

Jonathan blinked as the names rattled past. "Who has to watch it?"

"No idea." Manny considered. "Maybe just the husband? I mean, who else would want to watch a bloody show? I don't think *I* want to watch one."

Jonathan frowned. "But why? What's it for?"

Manny shrugged, mystified. "I don't know."

"Why didn't you get the rest of the information?"

Manny glared at him. "They all acted like it was completely normal, and I couldn't say anything, or they'd figure out I was listening."

Jonathan slanted a look at Manny. "Have you talked to Abby about any of this? She probably knows it already. She could put your mind at ease. Everything will be all right."

Manny looked away. "I want her to think I'm dependable, that she can count on me when the time comes. If I'm always running to her with questions, she'll know I have no idea what to do."

Jonathan laughed. "Why on earth would she think she can't depend on you? And, amigo, she already knows you have no idea what to do. Just talk to her. Stop worrying. You're gonna be a great father."

His missing dad flashed in Manny's mind. He didn't have a specific face in his memory anymore, only a vague impression of a tall, lean cowboy, much like himself, white instead of half Hispanic. *That's why she might think she can't depend on me. Blood is thicker than water.*

Abby's suffering took a toll on Manny. It hurt his heart to watch her move so carefully through the day, as if slowing her movements would trick her body into staying calm. He was helpless to ease her sickness. He racked his brain to think of a way to make her life easier.

The bathing room. He'd been planning to add on a bathing room for years but hadn't carved out the time or money. He would build the extra room for her and install a tub and a water system like he'd done for Yaideli. Abby would no longer have a hike to the outhouse. "Argh. Why didn't I think of it earlier?"

Early December's cooler weather was a welcome break from the sapping heat of summer, but winter was on its way. Come February, it'd be colder than a well-digger's boots. The babe would be only a week or two old by then. According to the information he'd picked up by eavesdropping, Abby would be sore, tired. She'd be grateful for the convenience.

His planned construction wouldn't be much of an imposition for her, and if he spent every free moment on it, he'd be able to complete the job before the child arrived.

Manny hurried through his chores of feeding the animals in the barn and mucking out stalls, then headed back to the house. He took a pencil to the rear wall and sketched where he planned to add the new room.

The sounds of measuring and muttering drew Abby outside. "What are you doing?"

Manny grinned. "I have a surprise for you."

Abby's gaze flitted back and forth between the scribblings on the wall and Manny's excited face. "What is it?" Her voice was guarded.

"I'm going to build that bathing room we've been talking about. You won't have to walk outside in the cold, and it'll be easier for you to bathe the baby."

A small frown pinched Abby's face. "You can finish it that quickly?"

Manny squashed the niggling feeling of discomfort, wishing once again he'd thought of it sooner. "Yes. And if I don't, it'll still be nice to have it when I finally do complete it. Either way, you get a tub."

Abby laid a hand on his arm, stretching up to press a kiss to his cheek. "It's a grand idea, and I appreciate it. Don't worry about hurrying. Maybe we should wait until after winter." Her voice quelled. "I know you have other chores to handle with the farm."

Manny shook his head, rejecting the slight sense of negativity coming through her voice. "The last of the hay is cut and stacked. I've got the wood pile built up. The new heifers are in a different pasture for weaning. All I need to do is take the rest of the bull calves to town to sell them. I have time to focus on this."

Abby smiled her thanks. "But you still have the animals to care for, tack to repair. You need to ride the fence. I don't want you to worry about some self-imposed deadline. We've been fine using an outhouse, and the tub in the kitchen warmed by the stove works quite well for bathing. We can continue the way we have."

"I don't want to just 'be fine.' I want to do better. You deserve the best, and I want to give it to you." Unspoken was Manny's certainty that he would be—that he *had* to be—better at this than his own father. He would prove to Abby and his son-to-be they could trust him.

Abby's concern didn't ease. "Can we afford it? We'll have extra expenses now with a baby. I'd hate for us to—"

Manny shushed her with a finger pressed to her lips. He ignored the annoyed look that flashed across her face. "Just leave it to me, Abby-girl. I'll take care of everything."

Abby sighed, watching Manny work so intently. He was like a little boy, seeking her encouragement. He seemed so happy planning the new room. However, she didn't fancy the idea of having the house turned upside down this close to the birth. Thoughts of cleaning, reorganizing, preparing the dusty crib Yaideli had brought in from her barn consumed her.

Yes, she'd used the tub at Yaideli's house. It would be nice once Manny finished the bathing room and installed one here. And having a stool and chamber pot inside, instead of trekking to the outhouse in the middle of the night, would be marvelous. But the reality of the mess she'd be working around each day made her grumpy. And the expense ... how much did a bathtub even cost?

She brought it up the next day at Yaideli's while the two of them sewed small sacques for the baby.

"How long did it take Manny to finish your bathing room after he started working on it?"

Yaideli pursed her lips, thinking back. "Hmm, *es posible* it was a few weeks, maybe three. Or four. It was a long time ago." She smiled at the memory. "It was worth the wait though."

Abby sighed, plopping the material she held into her lap. "I hate to sound ungrateful, because I know once it's finished, it'll be amazing and a great help."

"But …" Yaideli prompted.

"But I don't want the mess. I don't want the noise. I want to get ready for the baby."

"Ah, you're nesting." Yaideli nodded, her expression sage.

Abby's frown deepened with confusion.

Yaideli explained. "You want to make your nest. Curl up in a den like a mama fox and wait for the labor pains. Es normal."

"Manny's nervous." Abby leaned her head against the back of the sofa. "I can tell. I think he's so intent on building this room so he can compensate for something. I just don't know what."

"He does not know what to do, how to act. His *padre* was never around when he was very young, and then we received word the man was involved in a gunfight, probably gambling at cards, when Manny was five years old. Just never came home, the *patán*." She bit her thread off with a quick gnash of her teeth, eyes narrowing at the memory. "I think Manny is afraid of letting the babe down."

"That's ridiculous." Abby stiffened. "He'll be a wonderful father."

"Of course, he will. He just doesn't know it yet." Yaideli's look softened. "If you can stand the disruption, let him do this for you. He needs to."

Abby sighed again. She could stand it. She *would* stand it.

Chapter Three

Manny stood in front of the back wall of the Solomon Deutsch & Company store. Nails, wrought-iron hinges, cast-iron piping ... he stared into space, visualizing his list scribbled on the wall of the house. If he was to finish the bathing room in time, the construction needed to go off without a hitch. Was he forgetting anything?

A man stopped beside him. "Workin' on a project?"

Manny glanced over. Gabe stood next to him. His friendly question was all the invitation Manny needed. Eager to talk through his plans, he turned to fully face his new friend, describing the room he visualized.

"I have about six weeks before the babe arrives, which feels like plenty, but time is breathing down the back of my neck. I'm bringing my bull calves into town tomorrow to sell at market, then I'm free to focus on constructing the room."

"Hmm." Gabe rubbed the rough-nailed fingers of one hand over his bristly chin. "You're gonna be cuttin' things close. Maybe you should get some assistance." He paused, appeared to consider. "I could help you if you want."

"You have experience building?"

Gabe smiled, but it was small, reluctant. A feeling of sadness seemed to soften the edges.

Did I say something wrong?

The man shook his head, and his face cleared. "I do, actually. Built a house for my wife many years ago. Done some minor construction jobs here and there along the way since." He looked at the floor, mouth pressed into a line.

Manny stood silently. Gabe hadn't mentioned a wife the day he helped with the wood. Did she die? Had she left him?

Gabe's thoughts seemed to cloak him in gloominess.

When he glanced back up, his expression had calmed. The deep lines in his face were still there, and the bags beneath his eyes, reminiscent of a hound dog, gave him a sad aura. However, his gaze was clear, and he met Manny's regard steadily. "I can help you. Don't even need any money if you can give me a spot to rest my head at night and feed me three squares a day."

Excitement surged through Manny. Abby would be so happy to have it finished before the child arrived. A small doubt worried at the back of his mind. *Should I talk with her first?* He quashed the idea. Gabe had nowhere to stay. If he left him to return to the farm, the man might not stick around, could disappear by the time he got back. Someone may give him a better offer. No, she'd be OK with it.

"Let's go grab something to eat." Manny jerked his head in the direction of the Menger Hotel. "I'll show you what I have in mind. See if you agree. We can stop at the lumber mill and place an order before we head to the farm."

Gabe broke eye contact, glancing at the floor, patting his pockets with hesitation.

Manny noticed. "My treat, Gabe. My down payment for your help. Please, let me buy your lunch. You can help me iron everything out. I want to order the lumber today.

Gotta move on this. We usually get rain this time of year, and I want to take advantage of every day I have between now and mid-January." He clapped a hand on the older man's shoulder, his voice entreating.

Gabe straightened at Manny's touch. The small smile deepened, grew sadder if possible.

This guy is so lonely. He definitely needs to come with me. Abby'll make him feel right at home.

Manny headed to the farm with Gabe in tow, the sun hanging close to the horizon. They'd stayed in town far longer than he intended, but with the older man's help, he accomplished everything he needed to get the job started. The mill would have the lumber ready by the end of the week. He'd ordered the tub from the Watenhouse Department Store in Chicago.

Gabe's gelding plodded along beside Bosque. The purchases Manny'd made in town were loaded into the saddlebags, and more packages hung against the two horses' sides where they'd been tied. The man's horse looked as tired and worn out as Gabe.

"Think your horse can handle a cattle drive? I need to bring the calves to the market tomorrow. I could use some help."

Gabe leaned forward and gave the old animal a pat on the neck. "Buck's tougher than he looks. He'll keep up. We'll come along."

"Great. I'll get my friend Jonathan to help us. He needs to take his in also, so we'll drive the herd by his place and merge them into one."

Gabe tipped his head. "Jonathan is your age?"

"Yep. We've been friends ever since school days. The farm belongs to his parents. He lives there with them, helps with the work. But his dad became sick last year. He doesn't do much outside anymore. Jonathan took over the day-to-day running of the place."

"His dad won't come along with the calves?"

Manny shook his head. "No, he doesn't have the strength anymore. He's pretty much bedridden. He does the books, takes care of the money."

Gabe looked worried.

"I think we can handle the calves with the three of us." Manny strove to reassure. "His younger brother, Herschel, can come along if we decide we need more hands."

Gabe relaxed. "OK. I 'spect three of us can get the job done."

A farm appeared on their left. "Whoa, Bosque." Manny pulled his horse to a stop. "Hold on for a second. I'm gonna see if Abby is here."

Gabe peered down the drive. He made no move to follow Manny.

He sure seems skittish about meeting new people. Maybe that's why he's such a loner. Some folks just prefer their own company.

"This is where my grandmother lives. Abby is often here, working on stuff for the baby. But I don't see her horse." Manny looked around. "Actually, I don't see any of the animals. Or the wagon. Looks like Yaideli isn't home. Let's head to my place."

As they trotted down the long drive leading to Manny's house, Gabe studied the area. "Nice place."

"Thanks. I inherited it from my dad. It sat empty for several years while I lived with my grandmother, but I moved out here for good a few years ago. Started making improvements, turning it back into a farm. It's a great piece of property, almost five hundred acres. When Abby and I married, we combined acreage. Her homestead is next to mine. It'll be a good place to raise a family."

"That it will." A wistful look covered Gabe's face.

He must've lost his family. Maybe that's why he seems sad. Manny vowed to make him feel as welcome as he could while he stayed with them.

"You lost your dad?" Gabe's question brought his attention back to the present.

Manny pressed his mouth into a thin line. Lost him? Was abandoned by him was more accurate. "Yeah."

"What happened?"

He shrugged, a choppy, almost violent movement. "Who knows? He left me at Yaideli's to help in a cattle drive, rode off, and I never saw him again. The sheriff came by a few weeks later and told us a weak, cockamamie story about a gunfight. Wouldn't come right out and say it, but he gave us the impression he got caught cheating. Sheriff was too kind to speak the words out loud, though."

Gabe flinched. "Tough break. I bet that was hard on you, not having a dad around."

Manny shrugged again. "I was five. Don't remember much except he was hardly ever there. I don't know anything about him. Don't really care. Hard to miss something you never had."

Gabe was silent for a moment. "Every kid needs a dad." His sad look was back.

Although Manny wondered at the lack of details in the other man's story, he didn't pry. "Yeah. Every kid does. Yaideli played that role for me." He straightened. "Mine will get one. I'm gonna do the best job I can for him. For Abby. I won't be like my dad. I'll be good."

Gabe smiled. "I can see that."

They arrived at the barn.

"Well, here we are. Welcome to what will be home for the next few weeks. Put your horse in a stall. I'll go find my wife."

Abby looked up from the rocking chair, positioned to catch the warmth from the fireplace. Her knitting pooled in her lap. Manny stood in front of her, excited.

"I ran into Gabe again in town, Abby-girl." He was hopping-out-of-his-skin excited. "He's been drifting, taking work here and there, and he's in between jobs. He has experience building houses, said he built his own years ago when he married, and he offered to help me with the bathing room. Isn't this great? Now there's no way we won't get finished before our son arrives."

Abby blinked in surprise as her smile hardened into place. She struggled to recall the specifics of what Manny told her about his first meeting with Gabe. Based on what he said, her impression of the man hadn't been totally positive. She'd promised Yaideli she'd be able to stand the construction. She was wrong. She wouldn't stand this invasion. *How thoughtless.*

"You brought a stranger to our house? Now?"

She was tired. She didn't feel good. She hadn't brushed out the braid she slept in. She couldn't remember if she'd cleaned her teeth this morning. She probably looked like a porcupine and had the breath of a javelina. Now she had to worry about her appearance every day on top of everything else. And she'd be cooking for two grown, hardworking men, instead of one. Cleaning up after them. *Manny, you should've consulted me first.*

Yaideli's words rang in her mind, slowed her thoughts to a standstill. She'd promised to let Manny make a wreck of the house, but nothing was mentioned about inviting a stranger into their lives. She would try. She attempted an authentic smile. She pushed up from the rocker. "Well, where is he? Let me meet him."

The frown brought on by her initial reaction melted from Manny's face, and he pointed toward the barn with a big grin. "He's in here." He waved her on. "I'll introduce you."

They entered the barn, the interior dim after the bright sunshine outdoors. A tall, slightly stooped, thin man turned at the sound of their approach. He stood in front of the wall where the tack hung, one hand touching a leather strap. His expression was hard to read in the shadows.

Manny said he's a drifter. What if he's making a list of what he can steal while we're sleeping at night?

His face was a roadmap of wrinkles, deep ones cutting grooves on either side of his mouth like giant parentheses. Pouches sagged beneath his eyes. He swept his hat from his head. Longish hair—more gray than brown—fell in crinkled waves to his shoulders. The sun had beaten a ruddy color into his skin that wouldn't pale no matter how much time might pass without its rays.

A phrase her mother used to say passed through her mind. *He looks like he was rode hard and put up wet.*

He gave Abby a tired, guarded smile. One or two missing teeth marred his weathered good looks. He straightened when she approached, and his searching gaze traveled up and down her body.

She frowned and glanced at Manny to gauge his reaction. She reached up and patted her hair, uncomfortable under his regard.

Manny seemed to have noticed nothing at all. He motioned toward the stranger.

"This is Gabe. Gabe, please meet my wife, Abigail ... and my son-to-be." The grin broke into an even wider smile when he placed a protective hand across her protruding belly.

Abby shifted, embarrassed at the personal touch in front of the man. She couldn't resist Manny's enthusiasm, though. She laughed to herself, worries about the man chased from her mind for the moment. Manny was so pleased with the idea of the baby. His continual joy in the newcomer about to grace their lives never failed to warm her heart.

The tall stranger stepped forward, drawing her gaze back to him. Her smile dimmed as she faced him, but she swallowed her misgivings and reached out for a handshake. Something felt off about him. Abby couldn't rid herself of a sense of worry. A verse popped into her mind, one her father had often quoted. *Forget not to show love unto strangers: for thereby some have entertained angels unawares.*

She narrowed her eyes at the man, contemplating. OK. She could show love to him. But he was definitely no angel. His threadbare clothes, worn boots, and weather-beaten skin all proclaimed he'd lived a hard life. This one bore watching.

For now, she would stay out of their way and let them get going on the construction. The sooner they could finish the room, the sooner the man could leave.

Time will tell if he has ulterior motives.

Chapter Four

Abby turned away from the stove, pasting a smile on her face. Feet clomped on the porch. Manny pulled his boots off at the kitchen door. After a moment's hesitation, the man followed suit. She wrinkled her nose at the sight of his dirty, bare feet. His toes curled away from the chilly floor. He wore no socks. *I'm not getting near those boots.*

"We got Gabe set up in an empty stall. I put a pile of straw on the ground and covered it with a blanket. Makes a comfortable bed if you don't mind breathing horse toots all night long." Manny grinned, rinsing his hands at the sink, then lifted the lid on the cast-iron kettle with a dishrag. "Mm, something smells good. What're we having?"

"Venison stew. I used the last of the meat. You'll need to hunt soon or butcher a calf now that we have more mouths to feed."

The note of complaint in Abby's voice hung in the room, pealing like a church bell. Embarrassed at her rudeness to her unwanted guest, she hurried to cover the moment. "Please, sir, have a seat. Manny, will you finish setting the table while I get the water pitcher?"

The man remained standing near the door, hands tucked into the pockets of his dungarees, shoulders hunched. "I can eat in the barn, ma'am. I don't want to intrude on your family time."

Abby sighed and wiped a splash of stew from her wrist onto the apron that billowed from her body. Her belly marched before her like a town crier, announcing the babe nestled underneath the white cotton. "You're welcome to sit with us. Forgive me if I made you feel unwanted." She smiled. "I blame it on the baby. She makes me rather grumpy these days."

Manny laughed, walking past her with bowls and spoons in his hands. "Don't fall for it, Gabe." His voice teased. "She blames everything on my son. If only I had a built-in excuse like that."

The man tracked the banter between the two of them, his face softening as he listened to their raillery.

Abby caught the change. *Father God, help me see this man with your eyes, not mine.* The story Jesus told about leaving the ninety-nine to find one lost soul flickered through her mind. He would expect the same of her. She fought the feeling of annoyance. She didn't want to welcome him into their fold. What if he had the manners of a boar hog?

He moved to the table and sat. Taking a napkin from a pile stacked before him, he tucked it into his collar, smoothing it across his chest. He clasped his hands in his lap, looking for all the world like a youngster whose mom had chastened him for being naughty.

Manny sat, then reached for Abby's hand. "Let's pray."

She paused, then slid her other hand toward the man. He seemed just as reluctant as she but took her fingers lightly in his. She peeked while her husband prayed. Manny's palm clasped against hers, protective and warm, fingers interlaced. The man's dirt-encrusted fingertips pinched like a defensive crawdad, as if he were afraid to touch her.

The moment Manny pronounced amen, she withdrew her hand from the man's, placing it in her lap, where she wiped it surreptitiously against her apron. Manny leaned

forward, reaching with eager hunger to grasp the ladle, and filled their bowls with the hearty, aromatic liquid.

"Abby's a good cook." He smiled his praise at her. "I will say, though, it's a skill that has developed. When we first got married, I ate a lot of scrambled eggs and oatmeal."

Abby narrowed her eyes at him, then lifted her pert nose into the air. "You were welcome to take over the task at any moment." Her gaze twinkled.

Manny laughed again. "I never complained. Yaideli was an excellent teacher, and you were a very apt student. You set a fine table in no time at all."

She sneaked a look through lowered lashes at the man. He ate with quick intensity, but he wasn't sloppy. His hunger was apparent. He shoveled the food in like Abby might yank it away from him at any moment. But he wiped his mouth often with the napkin. *OK, not a complete ruffian. But definitely worse for wear.* What was his story?

He picked up his bowl, scraping the sides with his spoon. Abby grimaced. Would he lift it to his face and lick the remnants next? "Would you like a second helping?" She nudged the pot of stew toward him.

He peeked inside. He leaned against the chair rails behind him. "Oh, no, ma'am. Y'all go ahead. I'm full."

The words of Abby's grandmother, back in Tennessee, floated through her mind. *Never say you're full, Abigail. It sounds vulgar. Instead, use the phrase, "I've had sufficient."*

The man's gaze flicked back to the stew.

"Please, help yourself." Abby waved an encouraging hand toward him. "I work with tiny portions these days. Much of what I swallow doesn't agree with me."

The man hesitated.

Manny reached for the ladle and plopped a large spoonful into his bowl. "Eat up, man. Tomorrow, we work hard. We've got a cattle drive to handle."

The drive to town the day before with the calves had gone smoothly. Today Manny would take some of the cash he'd earned at the sale and pick up the lumber at the mill. Just after sunup, he walked out to the barn to see if Gabe was awake. The approaching dawn chased shadows across the yard. Mourning doves cooed from the eaves, and mist floated above the dips and swells in the pasture. Winter was on its way.

He pushed the barn door open and slipped inside. He peered through the dimness into the stall. The straw bed was unoccupied, the blanket folded neatly and draped over the partition. He turned in surprise, glancing around the empty space. Where had the man gone?

Outside, Sham barked, the sound friendly. Manny stepped back through the doorway to see Gabe shuffling forward, pushing a cumbersome wheelbarrow. He breathed hard, bringing a large, damp fieldstone.

"What're you doing?" Manny hurried forward to help.

Gabe waved him off. "Need some stones for the corners of the foundation. Been to look for a few in the shale along the creek bed. This un'll do for one." He pushed the wheelbarrow closer to the house. With a grunt, he tipped it and heaved the gray stone onto the ground with a thump. "Saw another one right near the first, but it was too heavy to carry both at the same time."

Manny blinked. *I didn't expect him to beat me to the punch.*

"Once we get stones for the other corners, we need to scrape the ground, make it smooth and level. In the past, I've had an ox pull a drum with a blade attached." Gabe glanced toward the barn. "Got anything like that here?"

Manny shook his head. "I can probably find a neighbor who has one."

Gabe shrugged him off. "Nah, it's a small area. It'll be more trouble 'n it's worth to travel all that way. We'll do it ourselves with shovels."

Manny stopped him as he turned with the empty wheelbarrow. "Hold on. Let's have some breakfast first. Come with me to the house."

Gabe straightened, his face unreadable. "Don't want to put out your missus."

Manny chuckled. "I've been fixing coffee and breakfast as often as she has these past few months. Let's go inside. If she isn't up, we'll handle it ourselves."

He slid a sideways glance toward the older man while they walked to the house. If Manny'd harbored any misgivings about this stranger's ability or willingness to work, they were long gone. Gabe made himself right at home with the project. A tiny flicker of shame burned in Manny's gut. He thought he might find the man snoring, expected to wake him to start the day's labor. The cattle drive had taken the starch out of Manny. He'd expected the same reaction in Gabe. But Gabe left him in his dust. Manny'd have to step smartly to keep up with him.

Abby woke to the sound of muted conversation from somewhere behind the house. She touched Manny's side of the bed without opening her eyes. It was empty, covers cool. She swung her feet to the floor and paused, perched on the mattress, taking internal stock of the baby situation. Normally, she would lie still for a moment, letting her body come to life in slow stages. But that man was here. She glanced down at her nightgown. This would never do.

No enticing aroma of coffee wafted her way. Manny wouldn't start the day without it, which meant he, and probably that man, would return to the kitchen at any moment to boil some. She swayed toward her pillow, tempted. She stiffened, tamped down her annoyance. Lazy wives stayed in bed while their husbands worked, but she wasn't lazy. Just a little queasy.

She stood. A wave of nausea swept over her. She dropped back down, then leaned over to grab the bowl tucked under the bed. The size of her belly made the movement almost impossible. The sensation of the baby pressing against her stomach made the gorge rise in her throat. She slipped to the floor and leaned her shoulders against the edge of the mattress. She arched her back to pull her rib cage up, allowing space inside her body for all its moving parts.

"Child, give me some room." She breathed as deeply as she could. "What will this feel like five weeks from now?" She touched her fingers to her belly, overwhelmed by the sensation of being carried along helplessly, an autumn leaf floating on the surface of a river.

A strong *thump* against her ribs made her smile.

"Don't complain. I live in this body, too, you know. Your papa is right. You're a bossy little tart."

The sound of the door opening pulled Abby's attention back to her surroundings. *The men are here.* She sat in a heap on the floor, her nightgown puddled about her knees, her braid a thick, fuzzy caterpillar hanging between her shoulders. A wave of embarrassment heated her face, followed quickly by resentment. At Manny for bringing this stranger into their home. At the man for intruding.

Manny poked his head around the bedroom doorway, his face alight with eagerness at beginning his project, obvious enjoyment shining in his eyes and smile. When he saw her on the floor, the pleasure vanished. Alarm flooded his countenance, and he stepped fully into the doorway.

"Abby! Are you all right?"

The other man moved within her line of sight, eyes wide with worry. When their gazes met, he blushed bright red, stepped back, and disappeared.

His obvious discomfort added to hers. Mortification clawed at her throat. Her answer was sharp. "I'm fine. Please close the door."

Manny flinched at her tone, hurt clouding his face. "What are you doing on the floor if you're fine?" He took a step toward her, offering a hand to assist her.

"Shut. The. Door."

Manny pushed the door closed behind him, then halted. He braced his palm on the frame. "Do you want my help?"

She sighed. She did need a hand, or a team of oxen, to help her up. She bit back her complaints and held out an arm. "Yes, please."

He stepped forward, grasped both of her hands with his, and tugged gently. He pulled her into his embrace and wrapped her in a hug.

She buried her nose against his neck, unhappy with her emotions. Their relationship had always been easy, loving. She was unsure why the man in the other room made her so edgy, so discomposed. Something about him put her off. But her husband seemed intent to have him there.

Maybe that was part of it. For the first time in their marriage, Abby felt slighted, set aside, replaced in his interest by someone else.

Ridiculous. The man was a complete stranger. *How petty can I possibly be?* She could share Manny's attention with another. *I've gotten spoiled, having him all to myself.* Naming the emotions surging through her helped. Surely, she could put them behind her.

After breakfast, the men hitched the oxen to the wagon and headed to town to get the lumber. Gabe sat silent beside Manny for several moments, shoulders slumped in his now-familiar posture.

"Seems like my bein' at your place is puttin' some stress on your wife. I don't want to cause any bother between the two of you." His gaze remained on the buckboard floor. "If I should move on, just say the word."

Manny shot a startled glance toward his new work partner. "You don't need to go. I embarrassed Abby this morning when I caught her in her nightclothes. I'm so used to coming and going as I please, it just didn't occur to me. We'll make sure she's up and about before we come inside from now on."

Gabe kept his gaze trained on the back of the oxen. "If you don't mind my askin', why are you so all-fired determined to have me stay? Your wife's feelings trump mine any day o' the week. And I can see from the setup you have on your farm, you're capable of building that room on your own."

An unexpected feeling of alarm washed over Manny at the thought Gabe might leave. The prospect of finishing the room alone rattled him. But it was apparent Abby would prefer otherwise.

Gabe was right. He could put the room together on his own, but Gabe *knew* how. He was confident of what to do next, had the steps planned far in advance. Manny was figuring it out as he went.

Awareness dawned. For the first time in their marriage, Manny was uncertain of himself. He didn't want to fail.

If his father were alive, he'd be by his side, helping him, teaching him. Renewed disappointment at his absent padre flooded his mouth with the taste of bile. Manny would never abandon *his* child.

"I need your help more than you realize." Manny finally spoke. "I didn't build most of what you see at the farm. My father did. I've been able to repair things, and I've added minor projects over the past few years, but I'm still wet behind the ears. Your help is very much needed. And appreciated."

Gabe gave him a considering look. A pensive smile quirked his lip.

The man hadn't talked much about himself, but apparently, he'd lost loved ones in his life too. There'd been a wife at one point. He had built her a home, yet he obviously lived alone now. Manny waited for his reply. Maybe the two of them provided something each needed.

"All right." Shadows lurked in the man's eyes, but his concerned look eased. "I'll hang around to help you, but you promise to let me know if your missus gets her fill of me."

Manny smiled back, relief filling him like bubbles from a cold root beer on a hot day. "Sure. She'll get used to having someone new around. Everything'll be fine."

Chapter Five

Manny strode to the barn carrying two steaming mugs. "Gabe! Got your coffee." The weather had taken a turn in the night, and the air was truly chilled for the first time since summer had waned. It finally felt like Christmas was near.

The room progressed nicely. The posts they'd sunk had planks nailed to them, and the new floor now sat waiting for walls. The wintery air was crisp with the scent of freshly hewn wood. Their first few days of work had done little to disrupt Abby's comings and goings. Banging hammers might disturb her, but at least the men limited the chaos to the outdoors.

Soon, however, they would need to cut a door through the kitchen wall. The installation of the tub and resultant plumbing would follow. Both men would be in and out all day long. Maybe Abby could stay with Yaideli when they reached that phase.

Usually, Manny discussed the construction project with Gabe while they shared their morning cup of coffee. Today, however, he had something else on his mind.

Gabe had shared minor details about his past while they worked side by side each day, and Manny discovered he'd had a son. The man would get as quiet as an armadillo playing dead if Manny asked questions, so he didn't dare probe about what happened to the child. Even though it must've occurred long ago, the man carried a sadness as heavy as a buffalo robe on his stooped shoulders.

However, since he'd let it slip he was or, at least, *had* been a father, Manny wanted to talk to him about the process. Finally. Someone with whom he could speak frankly. He was straining at the bit to see him this morning.

As usual, Gabe was already up and about. Manny had missed him again. He walked back to the yard and peered around. Where was he this time?

A muffled *thump* drew his attention. He followed the sound to the woodpile. Gabe had a foot-long length of log standing on its end. He drove a froe blade into the flat surface with the heavy strike of a mallet. Once the blade buried itself into the wood, Gabe twisted it toward himself by the handle, and a shingle neatly split away.

"Where did that come from?" Manny pointed at the tool, surprise lighting his face. Gabe seemed to carry all his worldly possessions in a battered canvas bag. He hadn't seen any hardware stowed away inside.

"Found it in the tack room." Gabe repositioned the froe and struck again. He added the shingle to the growing pile beside him. The fragrant spicy scent of pine filled the air.

"I owned that?" What other mysterious tools lived in the barn, waiting to be discovered?

"Either that, or Santy Claus dropped by a little early." Gabe grinned.

The appeal of his face struck anew as it did each time Gabe smiled. The deep lines in his weathered skin seemed less forbidding and sad, and more like the well-worn creases of a much-loved and oft-read book.

"Oh, here. Before it gets cold." Manny thrust the mug toward him. "Brought you some morning brew."

Gabe straightened, taking the cup, and slurping an appreciative sip. "Mm. Perfect strength. Where'd you learn to make coffee?"

"On cattle drives. I've helped with a couple to Kansas." Manny paused. Gabe had asked a question. Maybe it was safe to ask one of his own.

"I'm kinda worried about when the baby arrives. Do you know what happens? Were you there at the birth of your son?"

Gabe stilled, and a faraway look filled his eyes.

Manny held his breath, waiting.

"Yes. I was there. A midwife came. She had no trouble delivering him. We lived in an isolated area, so there was no one else around to help. They called me in to assist." He blew a cooling breath over the surface of the steaming coffee mug.

"What did you do?"

"Well, let's see. I had to boil some water, bring in some leather straps from the tack room for her to grip. My wife already had stacks of linens waiting—"

"What are the linens for?" Manny interrupted, his voice tense.

"There's a big gush of fluid when the baby is close. And there's blood after."

"Blood?" Manny's face blanched. His imagination's version of a bloody show flashed through his mind. Was this what they'd meant?

"You've seen animals born on the farm, right? It's similar. The afterbirth comes loose."

Manny nodded.

"The midwife said it leaves a wound inside, and it bleeds until it heals."

"A wound?" Manny's heart thumped uncomfortably. "Does it hurt?"

Gabe smiled kindly, crow's feet crinkling at the edges of his eyes. "It's natural, son. Every animal that births a babe goes through the exact same thing. Part of life."

Son. Manny looked away. His father should be here, not this person who'd been a stranger a week ago. His padre, teaching him how to use the tools in the barn that he'd obviously left behind. Explaining what to expect with the coming birth of his child. An overwhelming longing flooded him, something he hadn't felt, hadn't allowed himself to acknowledge, since he was a child.

He wanted to know what happened. Where was his father buried? Who killed him? Emotion clogged his throat, made it impossible to speak.

"Everything OK?" Gabe put his coffee mug on the upended log and took a step toward him.

Manny cleared his throat. Swallowed. "Everything's fine." He paused. "This may sound weird, and I don't mean to, but I think having you here, helping me, teaching me things ... it's made me think of my father a lot. Someone out there took away an entire piece of my life. Of me. I want to know what happened. Where he is now."

Gabe blinked. "I thought you said someone killed him."

Manny nodded, curt and impatient. "Yes. He got himself shot. What I mean is, where is his body? Who took care of that?" Frustration tightened his voice. "I can't imagine they just left him to rot on the prairie. It suddenly feels important to know these things. If he were here, he'd be passing the mantle of fatherhood to me. I want to put a lid on that chapter of my life. It's been waiting for a final nail to be driven all these years."

Gabe looked down, considering. "Who on earth could you go to? You said he died when you were five? Decades have passed. Do you even know where it happened?"

Manny straightened. "The sheriff. He's the one who brought us the news. He'll know something."

"Really? I met him when I first arrived. He's a young man. How would he know anything?" Gabe frowned in confusion.

"No. The old one. He retired. Moved to a ranch south of San Antonio. I could visit him, have a conversation, be back in two or three days."

Gabe straightened, ran a hand through his hair, leaving it in spikes. "You'd leave me here with Abby? I don't think she's gonna like that. You better talk this over with her."

Manny sighed. "You're probably right." He paused. "She could stay at Yaideli's. It would be fine." He looked off at the horizon. "What's in my ancestry? Who was my dad? What kind of man does that make me?" He glanced toward the house where Abby, with his unborn child, was in the kitchen. "I need to know."

"Well, maybe you do, but it doesn't seem like a great idea to do it right this second. Why don't you think on it for a while?" Gabe cautioned him.

"I'll ask her." Manny sucked his teeth with impatience. "Let's get to work."

Abby headed to Yaideli's, practicing arguments on the way. She flung her words into the space between Bird's ears, which bobbed up and down with each step as she pulled the little buggy. Low, gray clouds scudded across the sky, chased by the nippy wind that had picked up as the day progressed.

"Your dad has been missing for the past twenty years. You don't think there was, I don't know, *any* more appropriate time to go gallivanting off on a wild-goose chase than six weeks before your child is born? There's *nothing* more important waiting for you at home?"

She huffed with aggravation. Her coat fastened tightly around her body, the bump of her belly protruding from underneath the single button that held the two sides closed. Her breath plumed. Did an angry puff of steam also emit from her ears?

"Unbelievable."

Bird's ears faced forward as if she wisely kept her thoughts to herself.

"Yaideli will give him what for. He'll get a dressing down that'll strip off a layer of hide. How dare he even consider doing this now?"

Heartburn flamed at the base of her throat, and tiny heels kicked her insides as if the baby agreed with her outrage, registering her own disappointment.

"And he suggested leaving *that man* alone in our house. 'You could go stay with Yaideli if I go. She'll love to have you there.'" Her voice changed to a sarcastic, high-pitched tone, mimicking Manny's conversation. "As if I'm a child, nothing but an annoyance to be packed off to the closest relative. Stupid man."

She narrowed her eyes in anger. "We'd likely return to an empty house when he decided to come back home. Our new best friend would be long gone, along with the wagon, the oxen, and everything we own."

She clenched her jaw. "Simply unbelievable." Her outrage sat like a heavy lump of unrisen dough in her belly.

A wagon approached from town, a couple she knew from church heading out to the country. Their horses moved at a brisk trot. The man had an arm around his wife, holding her close to his side for warmth. They both smiled, and the woman waved.

"Good afternoon, Abby." She called in a merry voice. "Isn't this chilly weather fine? It's more like Christmas weather."

Abby pasted happiness on her face and returned the greeting. "It's wonderful, Cecilia. Y'all have a nice day now."

As soon as the wagon passed, Abby's smile pinched into an angry pout. "Must be nice to have a husband who *wants* to spend time with you instead of inventing reasons to disappear for days on end."

Bird turned onto the road leading to Yaideli's house. Abby slid her leg from the buggy, and with a grunt, her feet hit the ground. She pulled on the brake and stomped to the kitchen door.

"Yaideli?" She called out when she stepped inside. "Where are you?"

"*Aquí.*" The answer was muffled as if Yaideli's head was stuffed in a basket. "My room."

Abby walked through the house to her bedchamber. Yaideli had a large carpetbag open on the mattress. She paused in her packing to turn and look at Abby.

"*¿Cómo estás, chica?*" The older woman pulled her close for a quick hug. "Everything all right with the *bebé*?" She glanced at Abby's face, then frowned. "What's wrong, *nieta*?"

Abby plopped herself down on the bed, burst into tears, and vented her spleen.

Yaideli held her hand while she talked, patting it softly, like she was consoling a skittish colt.

"So, if Manny gets his way, I guess I'll be living with you for a few days." Abby wiped her eyes, then glanced at Yaideli, startled when no answer was forthcoming. "That's OK, isn't it?"

Yaideli pulled her hands away, then clasped them in front of her stomach. She drew a deep breath. "Nieta, you know, as my granddaughter, you are always welcome here. And you showing up here has actually saved me a trip to come tell you. I am packing to leave. *Tía* Rocio is very sick. I'm going south to Mexico to visit my family for a few weeks. It is likely she is not long for this world."

Abby gasped, her eyes wide. "You're leaving?" Her heart tripped in alarm.

Yaideli gave a tentative smile. "Sí. *Pero,* I need Manny to go with me. Es too long of a trip to attempt alone. There are Indians, outlaws, any number of bad people. Es about two days to get there."

Abby stiffened. "I'm coming too. Y'all aren't leaving me behind."

Yaideli patted her hand. "Nieta, you know it's not a good idea. You will be so uncomfortable. Sleeping on the ground. Bouncing along on that hard seat. You stay here. Everything will be fine, little one. The bebé will not arrive until late January. First ones always come slow. I must go. Manny will return in four days, five tops. He can stop to visit that sheriff on his way back. I will be home in time to help you with the delivery. Don't worry." She smiled sadly. "*Llamado de la sangre es fuerte.*"

Abby stared. She didn't care how strong the call of blood was. Yaideli and Manny couldn't leave her alone.

"Relax, chica. You look forlorn, like a lost, little puppy. No es *problema.*" She turned to her dresser and picked up a bag stuffed with fabric scraps. "Take this home with you and finish the clothes we've been working on. Time will fly by."

Abby reached for it, unable to form a response.

Yaideli's voice was reasonable, calm. "He will be back before you have time to miss him. And I will be away no more than two weeks. Once Tía Rocio has gone to Jesus, we will have a *velatorio* at the house for one day and into the night, then she will be buried. I'll have plenty of cousins available to escort me home. I'll come straight to you when I return."

"But what about Christmas? It's only ten days away. We always celebrate together."

Tears of grief shone unexpectedly in Yaideli's eyes.

Shame made Abby's face hot. She stood and wrapped her arms around her grandmother-in-law. "I'm sorry about your aunt, *Abuelita*. Don't spare another thought for me. I'll say prayers for her and for your family. And I'll go home now and tell Manny to prepare for the trip."

Yaideli stepped back and swiped her hand across her eyes. "Thank you for your prayers. Now I must finish this packing. I need to be on my way."

Abby headed back to the house. She tugged the collar of her coat up against her neck, hunching into its protection like a turtle. "I'm sad Manny's leaving us. Manny's sad he doesn't have a dad. I guess Gabe's sad about something too."

She stuffed her hand into her pocket with a disgruntled shrug. "God, will you at least bring him home quickly?"

Memories of her own parents flooded her mind. She couldn't really blame Manny for missing his dad, especially right now. His life was about to change, pushing him into a role for which he wasn't prepared. Was Manny feeling anything so different from what she felt? How many times had she carried on internal conversations with her mom during this pregnancy? At least she had Yaideli to help her, coach her, teach her what to expect.

Abby rubbed her belly. "Let's make a deal." She addressed her words to the child nestled inside. "You pretend you haven't heard every complaint I've made this afternoon, and I'll sing to you every single day once you're here. Agreed?"

By the time she trotted down the lane to their home, she had gained some mental equilibrium. She pulled Bird to a stop in front of the barn and climbed from the buggy with an ungraceful thump. She straightened with a groan, then turned at the sound of footsteps. The smile died on her face. It was Gabe.

"Here." He reached for the horse. "Let me take her. I'll put everything away and turn her out into the pasture for you."

Abby forced her unfriendly thoughts out of her mind. "Thank you." She looked around, searching for Bosque. "Where is Manny? I have some news for him."

"He's in the house."

Abby walked away without another word.

"Manny." She called his name, pulling her boots off at the door. "Yaideli has some sad news. Her aunt is dying. She needs you to take her to the valley."

Manny appeared in the doorway to the bedroom, his face somber at the news. Almost immediately, though, eagerness took over. She could see his wheels turning. "And you can stop in to see that sheriff on your way back." Her tone was disgruntled, but she couldn't help it. "Go ahead and get it out of your system. Just hurry home, OK?"

Chapter Six

Manny slowed Bosque to a trot as he approached the ranch house. He had delivered Yaideli to her aunt's house south of the valley with no problems. He spent the night, paid his respects, but left as soon as was feasible. He didn't know that branch of the family well, and the impending visit with the sheriff weighed on his mind. He'd practiced this conversation several times on the way back to San Antonio.

Several horses whinnied a welcome from the corral, announcing his arrival as effectively as a rooster welcoming the dawn.

Sheriff Williams walked out onto his veranda, squinting against the western light.

Manny dismounted, tipping his head toward the sheriff.

"Afternoon, Sheriff." Manny stopped short of the porch.

"Afternoon." The drawl was low, flattened of emotion. Instead of a friendly greeting, the man seemed cautious. He reached up and removed a toothpick from the corner of his mouth. "Do I know you?"

Manny pulled his hat from his head, revealing his scarred face. "You used to. I'm Manny Blair. I have a farm north of San Antonio. You came to my grandmother's house when I was young and told us—"

"I remember you." The man's gaze raked Manny. "Your pa was Mark Blair, got hisself killed at a card game. Sorry I had to tell you 'bout that." He stared, his face impassive. "What're you doin' here now? I'm not the law no more. Don't see how I can he'p you."

Manny studied the man. The word "sorry" may have come out of his mouth, but he looked far from feeling apologetic. Nervous? Maybe. A shiver of apprehension squirmed its way down his spine. This wasn't going like he'd imagined.

"Sir, I hoped to ask you some questions about that night." Manny twisted his hat in his hands, unable to control the urge to fidget.

The man huffed, placed the toothpick back in his mouth. "That was a long time ago, son. Don't rightly recollect much about that day."

But it was the first thing out of your mouth. "I'm trying to lay some memories to rest. Could you tell me where it happened—the card game? The shooting? Somebody must've buried him. I'm ... I'm about to become a father myself, and I need to put this to bed."

"I don't see how knowin' any of that can do anything 'cept cause pain. Some secrets are better left buried. I advise you to head on home and enjoy bein' a pa." The sheriff tugged his hat lower over his eyes, making them harder to see.

Manny frowned. Who said anything about secrets? When the sheriff had come to Yaideli's house all those years ago, he hadn't made the sad announcement of his father's passing sound furtive or mysterious. Men died on the frontier all the time.

The sheriff straightened as if he was returning to the house.

"Wait." Manny took an involuntary step forward. "Please, I'm not out to get anyone. It's not like I'm trying to cast blame and find a murderer. I need to know where they laid my father to rest. I want to visit his grave. Pay my respects."

"Murderer?" The sheriff gave him a hard look.

Manny swallowed. "That's just it." He stumbled to fill the space between them with words that would keep the man standing there while diffusing the startling tension that had built. "I'm *not* looking for that. I just need to ... to see my dad."

"Go home, Manny. I've got nothin' to tell you. That was a long time ago." He turned and started back to the front door.

"But where did it happen? Who else was there? Somebody must know something." Manny stretched out a hand. "Hold on!"

The sheriff slammed his door behind him. The distinct thump of a bolt sliding home floated across the yard. He stared, mouth hanging open in surprise.

In the sudden quiet, familiar sounds crept in. Cattle lowed from a nearby field. A horse snorted in the corral. From somewhere far away, a coyote yipped. The mournful cry reflected Manny's own dismay.

He jammed his hat back on. He whirled around and stalked to where Bosque waited. He pulled himself into the saddle and turned to leave. Glancing one last time toward the front door, he thought he saw a curtain twitch in the window.

"What in tarnation?" Manny muttered to himself, glaring at the front of the house.

What had started as an emotional journey now morphed into a resolve to investigate. His guard went up, like the ruff on a growling wolf. Was there more to this story? It sure felt like it, and Manny was determined to get to the bottom of things. He headed back the way he'd come. Maybe Jonathan or Abby would have some ideas.

Or Gabe. Perhaps somewhere in his checkered past, he'd made a friend or two who could sniff this out.

Resolution settled in his spine with the strength of the staff of Moses. "Father God, I don't know what that was all about, but I bet you do. You tell us the truth will set us free. Well, that's what I'm seeking, and I could sure use some help."

Abby sat at the kitchen table, taking small stitches on the diaper she hemmed. The rhythmic thump of a hammer outside told her their visitor was still putting up walls. Though Manny had left with Yaideli, the man continued building the extra room in his absence.

Abby had spent the entire first day holed up inside the house. She didn't know him, didn't trust him, and it wasn't her responsibility to worry about his feelings. He could stay, but he would remain outside. She prepared the evening meal, then placed his plate, along with a glass of water, on the back porch and shut the door firmly. Later, she opened the door to find a cleaned plate and glass sitting right where she'd left them, along with a fresh bucket of water from the well.

"Hmm." Abby glanced quickly around, but he was nowhere in sight. She stepped out onto the porch to check the progress of the room. He'd been hammering planks to the frame he and Manny had built, constructing walls, placing each new board so it formed an overlap on the one below. Two of the three walls were shoulder high. Sham lay on the porch and thumped his tail when she stepped around the corner.

"Are you helping, boy?" She touched the closest board. "How is he going to continue by himself once the third wall reaches this height? He won't be able to go much higher on his own."

At that moment, the man stepped out of the barn. He had a towel in his hand. It was apparent he was heading to the creek to bathe. Embarrassment heated her face. She stepped back inside the house and closed the door. After a moment, she cracked the door open and called to the dog.

"Sham. Come inside, boy." The idea of spending the night alone with that man only yards away didn't set well. She moved the dog's rug from its usual spot by the fireplace and laid it in front of the back door. He'd let her know if anyone tried to enter.

The next morning, Sham woke her scratching at the opening, whining with eagerness to go out.

"OK, OK. Hold your horses." She muttered at his insistence. Where was Manny when she needed him? "Taking stock over here. Give me a minute." Abby focused internally. Things felt calm today. Rolling to her side, she pushed herself up from the bed.

Sham danced. Did he really need to go, or was some critter sniffing around on the porch that needed killing? "Hang on, dog. I've reached buffalo status over here. It takes a second for things to get moving."

She walked over, pushed the rug out of the way with a bare foot, then opened the door. Sham shot straight out into the yard, where he barreled into the man, jumping and licking at him with wild abandon.

Abby narrowed her eyes. "Traitor." Her indignant mutter fell on deaf ears.

Gabe looked up with a smile, laughing at the dog's antics. She drew back, uncomfortable to be caught staring. She hid her body behind the door, toes curling from the cold seeping across the threshold. "I'll put some coffee on." She called across the yard, giving him a wave. He nodded her way, then continued to the woodpile. He was ready to start the day. She had to hand it to him—the man worked hard.

Cold air blew across her ankles. She shut the door against the chill. Instead of donning a dress, she pulled on a pair of Manny's pants, leaving the top button unfastened to accommodate her growing belly. His suspenders held them up. She slipped her arms into one of his shirts. It covered her almost to her knees. Thick socks warmed her toes. She fanned the stove to life and got coffee percolating. Quickly, she scrambled eggs and toasted slices of bread.

Abby shoved her feet into her boots and pulled on her coat. She stepped onto the porch, carrying two plates in her hands.

"Breakfast is ready." She called over the sound of the hammer, then set the plates down.

She went back for the coffeepot and two mugs, then returned to the steps. She sat down to eat just as he came around the corner. Surprise flickered across his face when he realized she planned to dine with him. She pretended not to notice. She wasn't quite ready to invite him in to eat with her without Manny there, but it felt churlish to continue treating him with silence.

He lowered himself to the steps at the far end of the porch, leaving plenty of room between them. Sham sat in front of her, using his pretty-boy pose to beg bites of food. She laughed at the soulful look in his eyes and relented, tossing him a bite of scrambled egg. He snapped it from midair, and it vanished with a gulp.

Gabe watched with a smile. "You like animals, don't you? You're kind to them."

Abby grinned. "I'm a softie. Manny didn't want Sham coming in the house, said he was dirty. So, I gave him a bath and brushed out his fur with the horses' curry comb. It was getting too cold to leave him out."

Gabe snorted. "He could've stayed in the barn. I'm warm enough."

She chuckled. "Oh, no. The barn is the territory of Silbida. Have you noticed her yet?"

"Are you talkin' about that gray cat?"

"Yes. She chased Sham out of there the first day he arrived. He got a smart little swat on his nose and came out yelping."

Gabe chuckled. "We've met. She comes and sleeps by me most nights. Makes a nice little warmer."

Abby's eyebrows raised in surprise. Silbida was fairly picky about whom she cuddled up to. "Really? I've never seen her get close to a stranger."

Gabe shrugged. "Guess I'm a softie too. Animals usually respond to me."

Abby studied him while he ate. Her resentment toward him was melting. "How are you going to reach to nail the boards at the top? Seems like it's going to be a two-man job after that."

Gabe looked over at the half-done room, rubbed his chin. "I'll figure out a way to prop up one end while I hammer the other."

A warm flutter passed through her at the gesture. It reminded her of Manny and made her miss him anew. Abby paused, then drew a deep breath. "I can hold that end if it will help."

He looked at her sharply, his shock clear to see before he shuttered it. "All right. I'll let you know when I need you." He handed over his empty plate. He tipped two fingers against his temple in a salute, then stood. "Back to work. Manny should return tomorrow. Don't want him to think I've been slacking. Thank you for breakfast. It was good."

"You're welcome." She breathed the words quietly to his back as he walked to his hammer, whistling a jaunty tune to himself. *For thereby some have entertained angels unaware.*

Manny's thoughts tumbled over themselves all the way back home, like rocks underneath a waterfall. His mood turned blacker the farther he traveled from the sheriff. He'd expected a few straightforward answers to his questions and directions to whatever mythical place the shooting supposedly occurred. He could've put this surprising obsession to bed, an obsession that seemed to have sprung from nowhere, and he would return to life as he knew it.

None of that happened. If anything, it was worse than before.

Manny eyed the darkening sky with a baleful glance. He was cold, dirty, and hungry. All he wanted to do was get home to Abby and talk about what happened. Then he would see what Jonathan thought he should do. When raindrops started falling, he turned up his collar and hunched miserably inside his coat.

"Don't this beat all." He muttered his complaint to the horse beneath him, whose skin quivered violently when the drops hit him. "They're not flies, Bosque. We're about to get soaked." His heels nudged the animal into a canter.

A sigh of relief left him when the road to the house finally came into view. He steered Bosque to the barn, dismounting with a groan, eager to see Abby and tell her his news. He'd check with Gabe, see if there'd been any problems.

He glanced into the stall where Gabe had his bed, but it was empty. "Hm. Wonder where he's at in this rain?"

He turned Bosque into his stall. He quickly pulled the saddle and bridle off and hung it in the tack room. He filled the trough in the horse's stall with oats and gave him a pat on the neck. "See you later, boy. Gotta check on Abby."

He hurried to the house. The sound of laughter stopped him in his tracks once he hit the back porch. Bemused, he pushed the door open. The sight that greeted his eyes was the last thing on earth he'd expected.

Sham leaped to his feet and bounded over, barking joyously.

Gabe turned from where he sat on the bench at the table, his hands held in front of him a foot apart, soft yarn looped around his fingers. Abby looked up with a smile, a ball of the fuzzy string cradled in what was left of her lap.

"Manny! You're back." She lifted her cheek for a kiss.

He walked over in a daze, pressed his lips to her face, then stepped away, his hand on her shoulder, inspecting her. "Everything OK?"

She cocked her head. "Of course. Why wouldn't it be?"

"What's Gabe doing in here? I thought you didn't li—" He bit off what he was about to say.

Her face changed. The smile morphed into a jutting chin, and her eyebrows shot to her hairline. She slid her gaze to Gabe, then back to him. "We've been fine. I helped Gabe build the room. We came inside a while ago when it started raining."

"You helped build the room?" Manny's eyes flicked back and forth between the two of them.

This was almost as unexpected as his reception at the sheriff's ranch had been. Abby had been very unsubtle about her feelings toward Gabe.

"Somebody had to. You were off God knows where on your adios-to-Dad escapade. This baby isn't going to fit inside much longer. We have a schedule to keep."

Manny met Gabe's gaze. The man shrugged as if to say *leave me out of this*.

"So?" Abby's voice pulled him back to her.

"Er, so, what?" He was on shaky ground and didn't quite know where to go for balance.

"Did you find out anything about your dad?" Her eyes widened, and she lifted her shoulders in question.

"Actually"—he glanced between the two of them—"things got a little odd."

Gabe frowned. "What do you mean, 'odd'?"

"Well, I want to talk to you about it." Manny pulled the rocking chair close to the pair and sat down, tugging off his boots and peeling away his damp socks.

"Me?" Gabe straightened. "What would I know about your dad?"

"Hopefully, we'll find out."

Chapter Seven

Manny recounted the story of his meeting with Sheriff Williams. Neither Gabe nor Abby interrupted him. After describing the twitch of the curtain at the window, he leaned back in the rocking chair and paused.

"I had plenty of time to think on my way home. I've run this through my mind over and over. Why did he use the word 'secrets'? Everyone in town knew what happened to my pa. He went to Kansas City with the cattle drive, probably had a packet of pay burning in his pocket, and got all liquored up. Sheriff made it sound like he mouthed off at a poker game, started an argument, and got shot. Common enough story. He didn't seem cagey about it when he told us the tale, and Yaideli has never been guarded or closemouthed about it to me. No secrets. So, why'd he say that?"

Abby frowned. "That does sound suspicious. But the sheriff?" She paused, tsked. "What would he have to hide?"

Gabe made a sound of derision. Manny and Abby turned to look at him.

"What?" Manny prompted him. "Do you know something?"

Gabe seemed to shrink into himself. "No. But in my experience, people aren't always what they seem."

Abby stared. "Have you met Sheriff Williams? Did you live in San Antonio before? You told Manny you were passing through, but you had old business to take care of." She held his gaze. "Do you know him?"

Gabe shook his head. "Life teaches hard lessons. I've learned some people don't live the lives they show the rest of the world."

Manny stared into the fire. "I 'spect that's true. I gotta think about this some more, see if I can make out what's behind that mask the sheriff is wearing." He slapped his hands down onto the arms of the rocker. "I'm gonna go check on the animals. Make sure everyone is settled for the night." He stood and pulled his boots on. The door slammed behind him.

Abby pinned Gabe with an unwavering stare.

Gabe picked up the yarn and met her gaze unblinkingly.

"Hm." Abby reached for the ball in her lap and resumed winding.

The hammering resumed the next morning. Manny was eager to finish. They had constructed all three walls. The room only awaited a roof.

Jitters assailed him. The two different projects now pulled his attention in opposite directions. He wanted to follow the scent of the mystery with the sheriff, but the bathing room took precedence.

"Should we put the roof on before or after we cut the doorway into the wall?" Manny looked to Gabe for advice. "If we leave it off, we'll be able to see better."

Abby wrapped herself in her robe and walked outside to inspect their progress.

Gabe rubbed his chin. "That's true, but it will also be open to the skies. If we cut a doorway into your wall and then it rains, your house is going to be damp and cold

until we finish. Even if it doesn't rain, it'll be cold. Let's go ahead with the roof."

She raised an eyebrow. "I agree. Roof first, please."

Manny grinned. "Yes, ma'am. It's your bathing room." He leaned a ladder against the wall farthest from the house and climbed up. Gabe handed him a board to create a rafter, and Manny nailed it on.

"Be careful up there." She wagged a stern finger at him. "My baby needs a papa. Don't fall and break your neck." She turned away. "I'll go make us some breakfast."

Manny climbed onto the board he'd just nailed, and Gabe handed him another. By the time Abby had breakfast cooked, the roof was ready for the wide, thin planks to create the ceiling.

The three of them sat at the table eating scrambled eggs, fried potatoes seasoned with onions, and pancakes.

"What comes after the planks?" Abby gazed back and forth between the two men, sipping her coffee.

"We nail on the shingles Gabe made." Manny gave him an appreciative glance. "He knows all the tricks. He found a tool in the barn I didn't realize I had and split shingles off a log just as easy as pie."

She looked at Gabe in surprise. "Aren't you industrious? How lucky you found the tool." She turned back to Manny. "And after that?"

Manny wiped his mouth with a napkin and leaned back in his chair, crossing one booted ankle across his knee. "We take the wagon into town and pick up your bathtub." He smiled at Abby. "It'll be here just in time for Christmas."

"The bathing room was a good idea, Manny. Thank you."

He glowed under her praise. He reached out and grasped her hand in his. "I want to make you happy."

She smiled back. "You always have."

A wave of longing and desire swept through him. The absence of intimacy chafed. According to the ladies at Hank's house, it would be weeks after the baby was born before marital play could resume. He sighed. Holding a babe in his arms would make all the sacrifices worth it.

Eager to put his frustrated thoughts behind him, he turned to Gabe. "Let's get the planks finished, then we can start laying the shingles. We'll go until we run out of daylight."

Dusk came early in December. With the dwindling of the thin sun rays, cold soaked into Manny's bones. The light from the lantern on the table inside cast a warm, rectangular glow through the window onto the ground. The smell of Abby's cooking drew him indoors as surely as a twitching string drew a kitten.

Chicken pieces bubbled in hot oil, their flour coating turning a tantalizing caramel color. Potatoes harvested from her garden boiled in a pot, while butter softened on the counter, waiting to be mashed in. The aroma of baking squash in the oven competed with the tantalizing smell of biscuits.

Abby turned from the stove at the sound of the door opening. "Getting too dark to see?"

Manny moved to stand in front of the fireplace and rubbed his hands together, stretching them toward the flames. "Too dark and too cold."

"Dinner'll be on the table in a few more minutes." She looked back at the frying pan and turned a piece of meat with a fork. "Wash up and set out the plates."

Gabe moved toward the table without hesitancy. "Is there something I can do?"

"You can fill the bucket from the well." She watched him step outside to do her bidding.

"He feels more like part of the family now." She smiled while Manny set the plates on the table.

"You got to know him better while I was gone." Manny studied her, watching her face for her reaction. "Seems you've reconsidered. You tried hard to disguise it, but I know you weren't thrilled when I brought him here."

Her cheeks flushed. "It's true. I've cursed you behind your back more than once in the past few weeks. But now I'm glad he's here."

He moved to stand behind her, placing his hands on her waist, bending to nuzzle the side of her neck. "Cursed me, eh?" He nipped at the skin just below her ear. "That's not very nice."

The small murmur of desire she made flared like a beacon in Manny's mind, and he enclosed her in his arms, sliding his hands to the sides of her heavy breasts. He stroked his thumbs against their softness.

Footsteps sounded on the porch, and Abby gasped, swatting at him and pulling away. With a growl, he turned and faced the table, struggling to gain his composure. He took a seat and placed a napkin across his lap. "Still glad?"

She snorted, biting her lip when Gabe returned. He glanced between the two of them, eyebrows raised. "Er, did I interrupt something?"

Abby sent a quelling look in Manny's direction and answered quickly. "No, of course not. Would you mind dipping some water into the pitcher? Manny, grab the glasses."

After dinner, they moved closer to the fire. Abby pulled out her ball of yarn and a pair of knitting needles and began working on a new project. Gabe pulled a chunk of wood from his pocket, then a knife. He whittled small pieces away, chipping the bark toward the fireplace.

Manny poked at the burning logs and added a new one. He stared into the fire for a few moments, then turned and sat in the rocking chair. He stretched his long legs toward the brightly flickering flames and leaned back, his head propped on his hands clasped behind his neck. He stared at the ceiling.

"What's going on inside that mind of yours?" Abby's voice was guarded. "I've seen that look before."

"When I go into town tomorrow to check on the delivery of the tub, I'm gonna visit the new sheriff. I want to know if he has an opinion about what old Sheriff Williams might be doing out there on his ranch. Something just doesn't sit right."

She narrowed her eyes. "Don't you go stirring up trouble."

Manny leaned forward, pointing his finger at her. "You know good and well you'd be digging around if it was something you needed to know. What if you heard news about those trappers that attacked y'all on the trail when you were coming to Texas? That they'd taken up residence nearby? You'd find out what was going on in a heartbeat."

She pointed her finger right back. "That was quite a while ago, and there wasn't a baby involved." Abby tilted her nose up in the air. "Things are different now. Just be careful, is all I'm saying. Am I right, Gabe?"

Gabe studiously looked at his piece of wood, carving like his life depended on it. "You may be."

Manny guffawed. "You'd just stand by while someone got off scot-free from something? You wouldn't even poke around?"

Gabe finally glanced up. "Sometimes it's better to let sleeping dogs lie."

Chapter Eight

Wagons, horses, and people crowded the streets of San Antonio. Gray skies blocked the late afternoon sun, though little warmth would come from the December rays. Manny grimaced, already wishing he'd completed his list of tasks and could head back home to Abby and the farm. Gabe had begged off coming along, stating he wasn't feeling well and needed to lie up and rest a bit. It rang false, but Manny didn't push. Looking around at the hustle and bustle passing him by, he acknowledged he would've done the same thing if he could. He'd rather be home playing possum too.

"Guess that's one thing we have in common. Both of us are loners." He reached down and patted Bosque's neck. "Let's get a move on, old boy. Gotta get down the street to the sheriff's office."

Manny tugged the collar of his coat up around his neck and nudged his heels into the horse's sides. They trotted down the dusty thoroughfare, dodging rumbling wagons, fast-moving buggies, and people darting through traffic. He coughed, the raised dust clogging his throat. The jingle of harnesses reminded him of bells. "Why does anyone want to live here in the middle of all this noise?"

He heaved a sigh of relief when the sheriff's office came into view. Dismounting, he tied Bosque's reins to the hitching post out front. "Don't leave without me." He slapped his palm against the horse's withers with a good-natured grin, then strode up the wooden steps, his boots announcing his presence to anyone inside.

Manny opened the door. The sheriff, a man in his thirties, and a deputy—an older man—relaxed, playing a game of chess. The sheriff had his feet propped on the corner of his desk, one booted ankle crossed over the other, chair tilted back on its hind legs. Both looked at Manny when he entered.

"Can I help you?" The young sheriff tipped the chair legs to the floor and stood.

Manny extended his hand. "Good afternoon, Sheriff. I'm wondering if I could take a moment of your time. I have a mystery I'd like to solve, and I hope you have some information."

"This sounds intriguing. I'm Sheriff Moore, by the way. I've seen you around town, but I don't think we've ever met." He shook Manny's hand, then turned to the deputy. "This is Deputy Hawkins." Manny extended a hand to him too. "Dean, see if you can rustle up another chair for us." He looked at Manny again. "Can I offer you some coffee?"

"No, thanks. Don't think I'll be here long enough to enjoy it. I just have a few questions."

Deputy Hawkins returned with the extra seat, and Manny thanked him, pulling it close to the desk. The sheriff gave Manny an inquiring look and settled back in his chair.

"This was before your time, but folks have long memories. I'm hoping you'll remember hearing something about this."

Sheriff Moore shrugged his shoulders. "Happy to help if I can."

Manny recounted the story he'd been told so many years ago by Sheriff Williams. He explained how he'd

become more interested in setting that part of his life to rest, now that he was about to become a father himself.

"Sheriff Williams told us my pa was shot and killed while he was in Kansas City, after delivering a herd of cattle to the stockyard. All I want to know is where the shooting happened, and if possible, who took care of his body after. I want to visit his grave."

"I can ask around to some of the old-timers, but I'm confused." Sheriff Moore frowned. "Why don't you ask Sheriff Williams? He lives just outside of town to the south, and—"

Manny held up his hand. "I already tried that. Got a rather strange welcome from the man."

Sheriff Moore frowned. "Strange? What do you mean?" He glanced at his deputy. Hawkins stared at Manny, his gaze impassive.

"Well, he seemed a little cautious. Nervous, even. Not real welcoming."

"Hmm. That is a little odd, but a man has a right to his privacy. What do you think, Dean? You worked with him. Does that seem out of character to you?"

Manny turned to the deputy eagerly, questions poised on the tip of his tongue. They died there. The man had his arms crossed over his chest, and the pointed stare Manny received was decidedly unfriendly.

Here we go again. What was with all the defensiveness? Hairs on the back of his neck raised.

"I think a man should have the right to live his retirement years in peace. Sheriff Williams devoted his life to this town. Not sure I take too kindly to his character bein' questioned like this."

"Well, now." Sheriff Moore's voice was a little too hearty. "Didn't sound to me like Manny questioned his character. Just making an observation." He stood, signaling an end to the conversation. "I'll ask around, see if anyone remembers your pa. Maybe we can come up with a location for you. In the meantime, congratulations on the impending birth of your child. God's blessings on you and your family."

Frustration tightened Manny's mouth, but he had little choice. He stood. The sheriff stuck his hand out. Manny shook it.

"We'll be in touch." A friendly smile softened Sheriff Moore's face.

Manny tipped his fingers to his temple. "'Preciate your time, fellas. Y'all have a merry Christmas if I don't see you before then."

He stepped outside. He swung into the saddle, glancing one last time toward the front of the sheriff's office. The young lawman leaned casually against the doorframe, thumbs tucked into his front pockets, hip slung out in a relaxed manner. The deputy, however, took a few steps toward the railing, like he was making sure Manny truly left. Giving him an escort out of the building. The back of Manny's neck tingled as he turned Bosque toward the post office. He could almost feel the glowering stare from the deputy.

"Well, I'll be dipped if I don't have more questions now than when I got here. If old Sheriff Williams and his pal, Deputy Hawkins, don't have something fishy going on, I'll eat my hat."

Bosque tipped an ear back as Manny muttered. They trotted away. It took everything inside Manny not to turn and look over his shoulder.

At the post office, Manny dismounted once again. He went in to see if the bathtub arrived.

The postmaster waved.

"Welcome, Manny. What can I do for ya?"

"Afternoon, Mr. Cooke. I'm here to see if my bathtub arrived from Chicago."

"Let me go check for you. I don't recollect seeing the stagecoach today."

Mr. Cooke vanished to a back room. Manny stood quietly, his mind on the conversation with the sheriff and the deputy. A bell rang over the door when a new customer entered.

The postmaster returned. "Ach, sorry. The delivery hasn't come through. You know, they try to get here every Friday, but things sometimes happen along the way. Maybe the coach will show up tomorrow."

Manny sighed. Both things he wanted to check off his list had been a bust. He wasted a trip to town.

"OK, I'll check in later. Thanks, Mr. Cooke."

Manny turned to go and almost stumbled over a woman. Her reticule fell from her hands and spilled open onto the floor.

"Pardon me." Manny reached out to steady the gray-haired woman when she squatted to gather her things. "Please let me help you." He knelt beside her, reaching for coins that had rolled away.

"I have information for you." The woman hissed her words, not looking at him.

"Excuse me?" Manny's hands paused, and he frowned uncertainly. Did he hear correctly?

"Don't look at me. Keep picking things up."

Manny slowed his movements, eyes trained on the floor.

"Meet me inside Solomon's in five minutes." Her whisper was harsh. "Back corner."

She stood. "Thank you for your help, sir." She spoke in a normal volume. "Sorry to be so clumsy."

Manny rose to stand beside her. He studied her face, trying to place her. She sent a bright smile and moved to step around him.

"No problem, ma'am. I think I ran into you." Manny's heart thudded heavily in his chest. What could she possibly mean? This day got stranger by the moment.

She walked to the counter. "Hello, Mr. Cooke." Her tone was friendly and conversational. "How is your wife?"

"Afternoon, Miss Williams. She's doin' fine. I'll tell her you asked."

Williams? As in, Sheriff Williams?

She obviously didn't want to be seen talking to him. Manny struggled to get his bearings. Who was she? And what did she know?

Moments later, Manny stood in the back corner of Solomon's. He inspected the goods on the shelf as if he would take a test over the contents on the morrow. Other customers milled in the store, and snatches of conversations floated over to him. He ignored them. His ear was attuned to the sound of one voice, and he hadn't heard it yet.

A person passed him, reaching for a bolt of ribbon.

"Don't look at me. Keep doing what you're doing now."

Manny stilled, a package of sewing needles held in his hands.

"My name is Carla Williams. I passed the sheriff's office right after you left. I overheard the deputy telling Sheriff Moore he needed to go tell Sheriff Williams about your visit."

"Williams, as in, the same family?" Manny kept his voice low.

"He's my brother."

Manny's heart gave a big ka-thump. He looked over his shoulder, checking to see if anyone else in the store had noticed them. No one peered their way.

"My brother is not a nice man, Mr. Blair."

Manny couldn't stop himself from glancing over in surprise.

"Look away, please. Yes, I know your name. I've kept my eye on you for several years. I think I have some information you'll find revealing, but I can't tell you here. Too many busybodies in this town."

Manny's head spun. *Several years?* Who was this woman, and what could she possibly know?

"You know where the boys like to gather on the river to fish?"

Manny nodded.

"I'll meet you there tomorrow morning. Go."

Manny turned and walked slowly away. Leaving with so many unanswered questions hanging in the air was one of the hardest things he'd ever done.

God, I feel like I'm in over my head. Please guide both our steps and keep that woman safe.

Chapter Nine

When Manny returned home, he sought out Abby. He found her behind the barn, pegging wet clothes on the line. A mockingbird kept her company from a nearby branch, running through its repertoire of borrowed songs. She turned when Sham leaped to his feet and rushed to greet him, tail wagging madly.

"You're back." She smiled.

Manny gave her a quick kiss. "How are you feeling today? Any sickness?"

Abby rapped her knuckles against the wooden post holding the clothesline. "Not so far. Maybe it's finally gone."

"Gracias a Dios." Manny reached into the basket for a wet shirt. The damp magnified the cold against his skin in the December air. He laid it over the rope and reached for a wooden peg.

Abby murmured a quick amen. "Did you learn anything from the sheriff?"

"I'm not sure."

Abby squinted, laughing. She curled her fingers into a tube and blew warm breath through them. "How can you not be sure? Did he have answers to your questions or not?" She tucked her hands under her arms.

"Not yet. Said he'd ask around." He reached for a pair of dungarees. "He seemed eager enough to help." He frowned.

"But it was a different story with the deputy. He's an older man, probably worked with Sheriff Williams back when he was in charge. He gave me a defensive, unfriendly stare. Didn't like the idea I was questioning his boss's integrity. They basically sent me packing."

Abby turned, the wet apron she'd plucked from the pile dangling from her hand. "So, the sheriff didn't help you at all?" Dismay clouded her face.

"Not so much. At least, not yet. Then something strange happened."

"What do you mean, strange?" Abby blinked, her gaze trained on his.

"I stopped in the post office to see if the tub arrived. When I turned to leave, I bumped into a woman and accidentally knocked her bag to the floor. I squatted to help her pick up what spilled, and she whispered she had something to tell me."

"What?" Abby gasped. "Who was she?"

"She didn't say. Not at first. She told me to meet her in the back of Solomon's."

"Did you go?" Abby couldn't hide the excitement in her tone.

Manny grinned. "What happened to this being a foolish search? You sound like you want to join in the hunt."

Abby slapped at his arm. "Just tell me what she said."

"She told me her name."

"And?" Abby stomped her foot.

"Her name is Williams."

"Williams? As in, *Sheriff* Williams?"

Manny laughed at her eager voice, then picked up the last item of clothing. "Yep. One and the same." He cut his eyes sideways at her, enjoying the moment, dragging it out. "Seems the sheriff is her brother. And"—he pegged another shirt to the line—"she didn't seem to think too highly of him."

Abby's eyes grew wide as an owl's. "How could you tell?"

"She said so. But that's as far as we got. She seemed very concerned someone might overhear us. I meet her tomorrow morning at the river to continue the conversation. And there was one more thing." He looked at her again. "She said she's been watching me for several years."

Abby stared, openmouthed. "Whatever for?"

"I guess we'll find out tomorrow."

Manny bent over and picked up the empty laundry basket. He took Abby's hand and walked with her back to the house. When they turned the corner around the barn, Manny almost ran over Gabe.

"Whoa, there I go again." The laundry basket knocked to the ground. "I can't seem to stop bowling people over." Manny reached out a hand to steady him.

Abby stumbled on the basket when Manny jerked to a halt. She peered over his shoulder to see Gabe's face. His gaze jumped around like a cricket in June, unable to light on a single thing. He wouldn't look Manny in the face.

"Um ... what are we gonna work on tomorrow morning? I think we can begin chipping away the wall to cut open the door. It'll take quite a while. Best get started early." Gabe spoke quickly.

Why is he so nervous? His normal, calm demeanor had vanished.

Manny didn't seem to notice anything different. "We'll have to get a late start tomorrow. I have a meeting in the morning."

Gabe wiped his hands against his thighs, a fretful movement. "This job'll be a long and difficult one. We'll start with an ax, then use a chisel and a mallet, and we'll chip away at the logs. I think we should begin as soon as we get daylight." Gabe pressed him.

Abby frowned. *He heard us talking. He doesn't want Manny to go.* A sudden fear bloomed in her chest. What did Gabe know? And why did he care?

"Maybe Gabe can go with you, Manny." She clutched at his hand, thinking quickly. The cautious sheriff, the unfriendly attitude of the deputy, a dead father, a mysterious woman whispering secrets. What was the thread connecting them all?

And Gabe. She looked at him. He could protect Manny, watch his back.

Manny twitched the side of his mouth, pondering. "No. Miss Wi—the person I need to see—is pretty shy. I don't want to chase her off by bringing someone unexpected. It'll be quick. Just a conversation. I'll be back way before the noon meal."

Gabe shook his head. "I think we should both stay here, get this finished. You want to be done before the babe arrives, don't you? No time to waste."

"Pshaw." Manny chuckled, waved his hand in a dismissive gesture. "A few hours won't make a difference. Come on in the house with us, Gabe. It's gettin' cold out here. We'll find something to do in front of the fireplace while Abby-girl fixes some dinner."

Gabe looked like he wanted to say something else, but he pressed his lips together. Thoughts chased themselves across his face. Was her own concern as obvious? *Father God, if Manny shouldn't do this, place an obstacle in his path. Thy will be done.*

Gabe took a deep breath. Abby held hers. Was he about to share information? Tell a long-lost secret? Confess something? Whatever came next out of his mouth held the potential to shake the ground beneath her feet.

He blew the air out with a puff of his cheeks. Abby deflated along with the air leaving his lungs. *What do you know, Gabe?*

If he had information that would protect the love of her life, he dang well better spill it. She placed a hand on her belly, shielding the unborn child from whatever unknown, unseen danger lurked. She glanced back at Manny. He had picked up on nothing. His excitement about the coming meeting blinded him to what was around him. Abby squared her shoulders. She and Gabe were going to have a little talk, and he *would* tell her what he knew.

After they ate, the men helped her wash and dry the dishes. Abby left the oil lamp burning on the table and added a candle to the mantel. The fire crackled merrily, popping and spitting when the sap inside the logs heated to steam. They pulled their chairs into a half-moon in front of the fireplace, Sham holding court in the middle. He lay stretched on his side, yipping a half bark quietly now and then, feet twitching as he chased something in his dreams. Contentment stole over Abby like a shawl, temporarily pushing the worries from earlier to the back of her mind.

She sat in the rocking chair and continued with her knitting project, which began to resemble a sock. She sent a furtive gaze to Gabe's feet, then glanced at her hands, comparing. Manny assumed his usual posture with his legs stretched out before him, crossed at the ankles, long feet making an X like the dasher from a butter churn. He massaged linseed oil into a small piece of calf hide. Gabe pulled out his knife and resumed his whittling.

Gabe studied the leather. "What're you gonna do with that?"

Manny raised his eyebrows and pressed his lips closed, a mischievous look brightening his face. "Oh, who knows? Maybe a surprise for someone's Christmas stocking."

Abby narrowed her eyes, sending an inquisitive glance toward the calf hide. He sent a cocky grin back at her, keeping his secrets to himself.

Manny cocked his head like a curious puppy. "What's that you're making, Gabe?"

Gabe's ruddy face flushed even darker. "Just a little toy for the baby."

Abby peered at the piece of wood, surprised pleasure lighting her eyes. "Gabe. That's so sweet of you. What's it going to be?"

"A push toy. He won't be able to use it for a while. Has to learn to crawl first."

"What will it look like? How will it work?" Abby leaned forward to study the wood in his hand. It had the faint appearance of a bird wing.

"If I do it right, it'll look like a roadrunner. When it rolls along the floor, the wheels will pull a string and make the wings flap a little." Suddenly shy, Gabe ducked his head. "It's nothin' really."

Abby clapped her hands with delight. "How clever."

She looked at Manny to see if he was as excited about the gift as she was. She paused. He squinted at the partially whittled toy. The studied look of concentration sent a flutter of awareness through her stomach.

"Manny, what are you thinking? You seem very serious all of a sudden."

Manny shook his head. "Nothing. I ..." He blinked. Shrugged. "Something was at the edge of my thoughts, but it's gone."

A Father's Gift

The night seemed to swirl with secrets.
Thy will be done, Father.

Chapter Ten

Manny led Bosque from the barn, then tugged the leather cinch one last time to ensure the saddle wouldn't slip. He buttoned his coat up to his neck and wiggled his fingers into a pair of leather gloves. He yanked the brim of his hat to settle it firmly onto his head. The weather had a definite bite to it this morning. He turned and found Gabe standing in the barn doorway wearing worry on his face like gloom, his hands shoved deep into his pockets, shoulders hunched.

He stopped, faced him full on. "Gabe, *tú estás preocupado*. Why? What's got you frettin'? Will it really be a problem if I miss a few hours of work on the bathing room this morning?"

Gabe opened his mouth and shut it again. He kicked at some straw on the ground. Finally, he looked into Manny's face. "Have you ever had a bad feelin' about something? A *presentimiento*?"

Manny narrowed his eyes. "Maybe. Do you feel that way now?"

Gabe nodded, the movement small and quick. "Can't explain it. Got no reason to back it up. It's just a nervous swirl in the pit of my stomach."

Manny considered, peering at him over Bosque's back, his hand on the horse's neck.

Abby approached and grasped the bridle. "Does *anything* about this meeting today feel wrong to you? Any warning signals going off in your brain?"

Manny scoffed. "You too? Since when are you superstitious?"

She shrugged. "God has spoken to me in many ways. Who's to say this isn't one of them?"

Manny gathered the reins and mounted Bosque. He settled himself in the saddle. "I think the two of you are off your nuts." He chuckled to take the sting from his words. "I'm meeting a person for a quick conversation. Period. I'll be home before dinner. We'll have the rest of the afternoon to work on cutting out the door. Then tomorrow, I'll ride into town with the wagon. Hopefully, the tub finally arrived."

He leaned from the saddle and gave Abby a quick kiss. "Don't raise a ruckus. Back before you know it."

He clicked his tongue at Bosque and cantered down the drive, leaving her and Gabe behind.

Abby watched him go with a frown, arms crossed over her protruding belly. Gray clouds scudded across the sky, low and heavy. They matched her mood. She turned and peered at Gabe. She said nothing. The cold wind rustled the leaves of a nearby live oak. A crow cawed in the distance. Abby let the silence between them draw out.

Gabe shuffled his feet. "I guess I'll—"

Abby held up a finger as if she were gesturing for his attention. She stared, her gaze direct and matter of fact.

The words died on his lips.

She pointed at the porch. "You'll bring yourself over here and have a sit-down with me. We are gonna have us a conversation."

"I have quite a bit of—"

"Now." Abby tilted her head forward so her gaze bored directly into his eyes.

He swallowed.

As genteel as a Southern belle, she gestured with one hand, inviting him to precede her.

He sighed and walked to the porch. He sat on the steps.

Abby stood in front of him, pulling her coat closed and stared. She stuffed her hands into her pockets.

"I have a confession to make." She finally broke the silence. "When Manny showed up with you, I was furious. I didn't want you here."

Gabe nodded.

"It was quite obvious, wasn't it?" Abby grimaced ruefully. "I apologize. I judged you unfairly, and I was mistaken."

Gabe leaned back, stretched out his legs as he relaxed.

"However, ..."

He straightened, a cautious look crossing his face.

"I pay attention. I notice things. And I have questions." She cocked an eyebrow. "Several of them."

Gabe said nothing.

"First, the day Manny met you, you told him you had *old* business to take care of in San Antonio, which is, I assume, why you came here. I thought at the time it was your first visit to our town. I assumed you were tracking someone down. Maybe someone owed you money. Now I'm not so sure. What is your history with this place? What was the old business?"

Gabe chewed the inside of his lip but said nothing.

"Second, you seem overly interested in Manny, in his life. I could've dismissed the growing friendship between the two of you as him seeking a father figure and you seeking to replace a lost family."

Gabe's mouth dropped open.

"You didn't pick up on that?" Abby searched his face for deception. "He hides it well, but losing his father affected him greatly. Especially as the baby grows, and his own looming fatherhood is staring him in the face. Then you showed up."

A flush colored his face. He glanced away.

"But your friendship happened so quickly. This level of familiarity is not ordinary for him, particularly when you consider how hard it is for Manny to make friends. So, my question is, why the interest? Why Manny?"

Gabe blinked but held his tongue.

"Third, I have a *feeling* about you, something that has tickled at me since the day you showed up. I don't know what it is or why I feel it, but it's there. Nothing bad, just *something*. And it bothers me." She narrowed her eyes at him.

He remained silent.

"Last question. I know you heard Manny talking to me at the clothesline. You heard him describe meeting the sheriff, and how the deputy reacted. And then the mystery woman who ran into him at the post office. That collision was no accident. I know it. And I believe you do too." She tilted her head and stared hard at him. "Right after that, you started dreaming up reasons for Manny not to go. Why?" Her voice was hard. "What do you know?"

Gabe broke eye contact and looked at her feet.

"Gabe, if you know something, you must tell me." For the first time, Abby's stern voice broke. "Is my husband walking into trouble?" Fear trembled in her throat. "Please don't look away from me. Don't lie. He is my whole life. I can't lose him. Is he in danger?"

Gabe glanced back up.

Abby pinned him to the porch with her gaze. "What do you know?"

A Father's Gift

Manny slowed when he approached the bend in the river where the local boys liked to fish. The sun struggled to break through clouds. Ducks paddled toward the other bank as he neared, leaving ever-widening ripples in their wake. Excitement thrummed through his veins. What would the woman say? Did she know something about his father?

Bosque whinnied. Manny gazed around, then spotted Miss Williams when she nudged her horse from her spot in the trees.

He raised a hand in greeting as she neared him.

"Follow me." She turned back toward the grove of live oaks and concealed herself within their somber black trunks.

Manny trailed behind, biting down on his impatience.

Finally, deep within the copse, she pulled her horse to a stop. "Thank you for coming. I wasn't sure you would."

He smiled. "I think if my wife'd had her way, I wouldn't be here. It was all a little too mysterious for her taste."

"You sound like this is a game I'm playing with you." Her tone was harsh. "I assure you, this is deadly serious."

Manny swallowed. He waited for her to speak.

"Allow me to fill in some history. Twenty-five years ago, I fell in love with a man named Luis Rodriguez. He was Mexican, and his family had lived in Texas since before Santa Anna took the Alamo. The execution of the Texas soldiers at the mission bred a hatred for Mexicans in the folks who lived here." She made a sharp movement of negation with her head.

"The battles with the Mexican army didn't matter to me. Luis had nothing to do with any of that. He was a *vaquero*.

He raised cattle. But Santa Anna's horrible treatment of the Texan soldiers permanently altered people's perceptions. The Texas Rangers stationed here made it their personal mission to kill every Mexican soldier they found."

Her horse shifted, swished his tail. She stroked his neck, lost in her memories. With a sad smile on her face, she looked at Manny.

"My brother, Rusty—you know him as Sheriff Williams—was a ranger before he became sheriff. The particular ranger company he joined was little more than a bloodthirsty militia with a taste for revenge. They went rogue, did what they wanted, killed whomever they felt like killing, raped and robbed as they cut their swath through the Texas wilderness. They were practically criminals, but they were largely unsupervised, and the government needed rangers to protect the families on the frontier. First, from Indians. And then from Mexicans. People here treated them like heroes. Maybe they were at times. I think the power corrupted Rusty, gave him the sense he was above the law."

Manny bit back questions he wanted to ask.

"When Rusty found out Luis proposed to me, he lost his mind. He called me horrible names, made unspeakable accusations about me, about Luis. He told me no blood of his would ever marry a greaser. Over his dead body, he said."

A sick feeling settled in Manny's stomach.

"My Luis left to help take a herd of cattle to Kansas City. He told me we'd use the money he earned to buy more land, build a house. We'd be true *rancheros*." Miss Williams looked away, eyes misty. "I never saw him again."

Manny lifted his hand as if to reach for her, then placed it on the saddle horn. Awkwardness flooded him.

"I know Rusty had something to do with his disappearance. He came to me, hat in hand, saying he was sorry to tell me Luis stayed in Kansas City, that he wasn't coming home. Said he sent a message, saying he didn't love me, told me to move on with my life." Her eyes were desolate. "But my brother wasn't sorry. His words said it, but his face didn't. His eyes didn't."

Manny thought back to what the sheriff said to him. The exact thought had crossed his own mind. *Your eyes didn't match your words.* "I'm sorry for your loss, but what does this have to do with me?" Strands of truth began weaving around Manny like the silky threads of a spider's web, but he couldn't quite see the pattern.

"Luis knew your father."

The bottom fell out of his stomach. *Finally, someone with knowledge.*

"I think your father went on the cattle drive with my fiancé. I'm almost certain Rusty killed Luis. The hatred, stirred on by his time with the rangers, had settled in his heart. He couldn't bear to think of our family line being *sullied*." The bitterness in her voice reflected in her twisted face. "If he killed Luis, and if Mark was there, saw it, or somehow learned the truth, maybe he killed your father too."

Manny's throat closed.

The web began forming around him. A picture emerged.

Crocodile tears on the man's face when he delivered the news twenty years ago.

Your father cheated at cards.

Drunk.

Gunned down.

And false sympathy twenty years later.

I can't help you, Manny.

Some secrets are better left buried.

"He killed my pa?" The words would hardly come.

This time, it was Miss Williams who reached out. Her hand gripped his wrist. Empathy shone in her eyes. "We'll probably never know for sure. The murder happened a long ago, and he probably thinks he's in the clear after all these years. The chances of finding someone who was on that cattle drive, who saw what happened, who is still alive to talk ... well, this scenario is doubtful. But that's not why I asked you here."

Manny shook his head, clearing the fuzzy confusion, rage emerging like the head of a seedling poking up through the dirt. "What do you mean?"

"Dean Hawkins worked with my brother the whole time he was sheriff. I think Dean was a Texas Ranger with him. Which means he was right there by his side while he was killing Indians and Mexicans. They've been in cahoots from the get-go. I cannot fathom Dean would blow on Rusty. Any secrets my brother had, Dean would keep."

"So?" Manny frowned. "What are you saying?"

"I told you I passed by right after you left Sheriff Moore. I heard Dean say he was heading out to Rusty's. If I'm right, and my brother killed my intended and, possibly, your father, he is now on notice that you're asking questions. I know he's killed more men than he can remember, but they were Mexicans. In his mind, they don't count. He believes no one would blink an eye if that came out and people knew the truth. But ... if you made it known that Rusty killed a white man, one of their own ..."

Awareness of the potential danger washed down Manny's spine like a bucket of cold water.

"If Rusty wanted to know where you lived, he'd have the information in two shakes of a lamb's tail."

Abby. The baby.

That monster might be on his way to town as they spoke, seeking information about where the farm lay. Williams knew where Yaideli lived but had never been to the Blair homestead. Manny had to head him off. But what would he do with him if he found him?

Take him to the sheriff? Deputy Hawkins would be there to turn him loose the moment the opportunity presented itself.

Have a shootout in the street? He couldn't gun a man down in cold blood.

God, what do I do? Protect Abby and the baby, please. Send your angels.

Miss Williams dismounted and walked to an old oak tree. She stroked her hand across the bark. An intense spasm of grief passed across her face. Manny looked at the trunk. A rough carving of a heart displayed a weather-beaten message. The tip of her index finger traced the letters on top. Manny read "... loves C. M. W." in the bottom part of the heart.

"Did Luis carve that?" Manny asked the question gently.

"Yes." Her smile was sad.

"What does the M stand for?"

"Mae. Named for my mother."

She dropped her hand to her side, revealing the initials of her lost love.

L. G. R. G.

"And those initials? Obviously, the L stands for Luis. What's the rest?"

"Luis Gabriel Rodriguez Galindo." She said his name with reverence.

Manny frowned.

Gabe?

Chapter Eleven

Manny spurred Bosque into a mile-eating gallop on the dusty road, heading into town as if the devil himself nipped his heels.

Angry thoughts tumbled in his mind as busy as a kicked anthill. Did the sheriff murder his father? Apparently, there was no drunken card game. His dad had *not* been gambling or womanizing. He'd been on a cattle drive. This changed everything he knew about his father.

So, who were the players in the scene?

Main character—the father. Mark Blair.

Villain—the retired sheriff. Rusty Williams.

Villain's sidekick—the deputy. Dean Hawkins.

Possible good guy—the current sheriff. Sheriff Moore.

Mysterious stranger—the woman in the post office. Carla Williams.

Tragic victim—the murdered fiancé. Luis Gabriel Rodriguez Galindo.

And Gabe. What role did Gabe play?

It was too coincidental that someone named Gabriel was Mark Blair's friend, and then a man named Gabe appeared out of nowhere to play a part in his life. How was Gabe connected to Gabriel? A triangle appeared where none should exist.

Manny ran the conversation with Sheriff Williams through his mind. *Some secrets are better left buried.* He hadn't realized there *were* secrets. If Carla Williams was trustworthy, and he had no reason to believe she wasn't, the old sheriff had a big secret. He murdered someone. Maybe two someones.

His meeting with Sheriff Moore resurfaced in his mind. What did he know about William's past?

A single fact sat as unavoidable as a brightly glowing campfire in the middle of a wild, dark prairie: Deputy Hawkins left to tell Sheriff Williams Manny was asking questions.

The deputy hid the sheriff's secrets for two decades. And he was on his way to see a person accused of cold-blooded murder. To have a chat. About him.

Some secrets are better left buried.

"What do I do, God?" He snorted. "I'm angry. If Williams killed my father ..." Heat surged through his veins. He clenched his hands. "I'm almost to town, riding straight toward danger. Now what?"

All too soon, Bosque trotted down Soledad. Manny swallowed hard. He pushed the thoughts of vengeance as far down as he could. A clear mind was critical. He straightened when he turned onto Commerce. He tugged his hat brim low over his eyes. Clenched his jaw. He scanned the road in front of him. Where was Williams? Had the man come to town after his visit from Hawkins?

As he passed Sheriff Moore's office, he glanced into the open door. A man stood. Walked to the sidewalk. The deputy. Manny tamped down the flare of anger that surged at the thought of his cover-up. Twenty-plus years was a long time to hinder justice.

The deputy leaned his shoulder against the doorjamb, crossed his legs at the ankle, tucked his thumbs into his pockets. A toothpick dangled with languid carelessness from the corner of his mouth.

Miss Williams said Hawkins went out to her brother's ranch yesterday. It must have been a hard, quick trip for him to get out there and back again in one day.

Or maybe he didn't go. Maybe all of this was nothing more than the fevered imaginings of a lovelorn woman inventing reasons to excuse the abandonment of her lover.

Maybe Manny kicked a hornets' nest for no good reason. Why stir up the animosity of a powerful man, create an enemy? He should go home, talk to Gabe. This was silly. He pulled on Bosque's reins.

Hawkins's hard eyes had the look of a hunter assessing a target.

Then Manny saw the horses tied to the hitching post in front of the saloon. All three wore the Williams brand on their hindquarters. Three of the man's horses, here in town.

The twinned batwing doors of the saloon swung open. Williams, flanked by calloused ranch hands, walked out onto the wooden sidewalk. He looked at Manny but said nothing. He walked to his horse and untied the reins. He swung up into the saddle. The men with him followed suit.

Anger bloomed again. *Did you kill my dad?*

Manny glanced behind him. Hawkins had mounted and he approached, his horse walking with a leisurely pace, but his eyes didn't match the easygoing stride of the animal. They were predatory.

OK, God. I came here to find him. Now what?

He couldn't go home. He would lead the four men straight to Abby and the baby. He could continue through town until he reached the outskirts at the southern end. But then he'd be alone with them, all of whom were armed.

He eyed the three horses. Each saddle had a rifle scabbard tied on. All held a weapon. Surely, Williams wouldn't be brazened enough to pull on him in the middle of town, with innocent bystanders there to witness his deed. No, staying inside the city limits was probably safest, but Manny had to confront the man. He couldn't stay here all day. He had to return home at some point. He nudged Bosque back into motion. He kept his eyes trained on the road ahead.

To buy some time, Manny pulled Bosque to a stop in front of Leopold's Dry Goods. He'd go in, pretend to buy Abby a card of ribbon. Maybe a brilliant solution would present itself.

He dismounted and wrapped the reins around the hitching post. When his foot hit the last step to the sidewalk, something hard pressed against his ribs, and a heavy hand clamped onto his shoulder. He stiffened.

"Howdy, friend." Williams's voice spoke in Manny's ear. "I believe a conversation is in order. Won't you accompany my pals and me?"

Manny stopped, clenched his teeth over the accusations he wanted to fling. His fingers curled into fists, nails pressing half-moon sickles into his palms. "Sorry, I can't. I was just heading into—"

The pressure on his ribs became the sharp jab of a pistol. "Wasn't really askin', Manny. Just come along."

Abby stared Gabe down. He wouldn't get up until she got answers. Sham ambled over and flopped onto the porch beside him. He licked one paw, then stretched out and closed his eyes with a sigh. Abby pasted a smile on her face and sighed also. "I need an explanation. And, just like Sham, I'm prepared to wait you out."

Gabe rubbed his chin. "Abby, I can't help you. I don't live in San Antonio. I don't know these people."

She narrowed her eyes. "You said you had old business to take care of. What's that about?"

"I spent a little time here years ago. I had a run-in with a fella, but I left before settling accounts. It seemed the prudent thing to do at the time, but life has a way of circling around on you till you straighten things out. I returned to wrap up loose ends."

"So, have you? Wrapped up loose ends?"

Gabe shrugged. "Not just yet. But I think things are coming to a head."

"Things involving Sheriff Williams? Come clean, Gabe." Abby pointed a finger at him. "It's clear as the nose on your face you know something about him."

He opened his mouth. Shut it. "I ..." He paused. "Abby, my methods of clearing up my past may place me on the wrong side of the line between right and wrong. I don't want to involve you or Manny in that."

At her startled look, he reached out his hands, palms up. "I'm not gonna murder anyone. Nothing like that. But it might get ugly, and I'd rather not drag anyone into my troubles."

"So, your interest in Manny is coincidental?"

"He's just a guy I met on the side of the road who needed a hand." He shrugged again. "I like him. He's nice. He'll be a great dad. But that's all."

"Why'd you get all interested in his affairs after you eavesdropped? When you heard the name Carla Williams, you started coming up with excuses to keep him at home."

"I remember Carla Williams." Gabe looked off into the distance. "At least, I think I do. She was close to my age."

"Why'd her name get you so fired up?" Abby pressed hard. She wanted answers.

Gabe shook his head, looked at the ground. "Abby, I can't drag you into this. Please believe me. I won't do anything that might put you or Manny in danger. To do that, I need to keep what I know to myself. At least for now."

Abby glared. *God, do I trust him? Is he good?* She straightened, suddenly weary. She dug her fist into the small of her back.

"I'm tired of trying to figure this out. You. Manny. All these secrets." She huffed with exasperation. "I'm cold and I'm going inside. I'll start dinner soon. I guess you can get things ready to work on the room while we wait for Manny." She snapped her fingers at Sham as she climbed the porch steps. "Come on, boy."

Abby ran Gabe's conversation through her mind while she stitched on the baby clothes. He knew the old sheriff, and he knew Carla Williams. The sheriff had secrets, too, it appeared. Now Manny was involved. She sighed. The whole thing made her tired.

When Manny returned, the three of them would sit down and go through everything from the beginning. Lay it all out on the table. Whatever Manny learned from the meeting with Carla Williams would surely shed some light. She glanced at Sham. "Maybe Manny can get Gabe to spill his guts. God knows, I'm getting nowhere."

She twisted at the waist, groaned. "Argh. Everything hurts today. I'm going to lie down for a little bit." She petted Sham on the head when she stood and headed to the bedroom.

What seemed like moments later, she awoke, disturbed by Sham's barking. She rolled to her side and swung her feet to the floor. "What is it, boy? Is Manny home?" She shuffled to the back door and pulled it open, letting the dog outside. Instead of racing out to leap onto Gabe, he stood at the steps and barked. Abby frowned. She looked around. Gabe was nowhere in sight. No hammering sounds disturbed the calm of the afternoon.

A Father's Gift

"What time is it?" Abby studied the sky, surprised to see the sun was farther along than she expected. It was well past noon. Where were the men? Manny said he'd be home for dinner.

She walked to the barn, followed by Sham, and entered the warmth of its dim interior, expecting to see them doing something in the tack room with tools. The barn was empty. Alarm caused her heart to leap to her throat. She glanced around wildly. Surely, she'd missed seeing a horse or two in the shadows.

No Bosque. Manny hadn't come back.

No Buck. Gabe was gone.

"Oh, dear God. What now?"

She turned. Should she hitch Bird to the buggy and head to town? Apparently, everyone else was there. Might as well join the party.

She walked to the tack room and reached for a harness. A sudden pain cramped through her abdomen. She gasped. Sham perked his ears and gave a quick yip.

"What the heck was that?" Abby rubbed her palm on her belly. No more pains attacked, just the dull ache in her back that wouldn't subside.

"It's OK, Sham. I think all is well. But maybe I shouldn't go to town after all. Let's go make a hot tea."

She turned to head out of the barn, then cried out. Dampness spread down her legs.

"Oh, my God. My water just broke."

Chapter Twelve

Manny's thoughts raced. Williams slung his arm around his neck like they were long-lost pals. He hustled him down the wooden sidewalk toward an alley at the end of Commerce Street. The two ranch hands followed, their bodies shielding what happened from any curious gazes.

He caught me flat-footed. I made a greenhorn's mistake.

Williams shoved Manny from the wooden platform when they reached the end of the sidewalk. He stumbled, almost dropping to his knees. Williams jumped lightly to the ground beside him, taking up the same position he had before. The barrel of the gun poked again, insistent. Manny straightened. A river of ice ran down his back. A buckboard wagon waited in the alley. A cowboy sat patiently on the driver's bench. The sight that chilled Manny was the canvas tarp pooled in the wagon.

Perfect for hiding a body.

If he walked down that alleyway, he'd sign his own death warrant. He dug in his heels.

Hawkins caught the motion. He laughed.

"Looks like the little dogie doesn't wanna go, Rusty. Better handle him like we do the calves. Get out the lariat, Tommy." He called to the man waiting in the alley.

The cowboy stood and reached behind him. He pulled a coiled length of rope from the wagon. He shook out a large loop, cradling the rest of the line in a coil. Slowly and deliberately, he swung the lasso around his head. Manny watched the lariat circle through the air with the hypnotic effect of a magician's wand.

If that rope settled around his torso, the cowboy would yank it tight. The lasso would pin Manny's arms to his rib cage. They'd likely jerk him from his feet and drag him to his death behind the wagon. The sheriff could always say Bosque spooked at a snake and threw Manny from the saddle. A dragging death by a stampeding horse was not so uncommon, one boot snagged in the stirrup.

A picture of Abby flashed through his mind. In his imagination, she cuddled their baby, a thick braid hanging over her shoulder, her face leaning down, beaming with love. He couldn't leave her to raise his son alone.

Manny swallowed and drew a fortifying breath. He stood one against five. It would never work. It had to work.

When you're for me, who can be against me?

Manny funneled anger into his arm. He jabbed his elbow into Williams's rib cage with as much strength as he could muster. A pained "oomph" grunted into his ear. He shrugged his shoulder violently, knocking Williams's hand away.

"You won't shoot me right here on the sidewalk. Look around you, man. People are staring." Manny's voice shook with anger. "They'll also notice if you rope me like a calf needing branding. What's your intention?" He faced him full on. "Did you really shoot and kill a defenseless man all those years ago? You plan to do it again?"

Williams's face blanched. *Ah. He didn't like that.* His discomfort fueled Manny's courage.

"Boss, whaddya want us to do?" The two ranch hands stood by, arms held away from their sides, fingers twitching like they itched to pull a gun. Their gazes flicked back and forth between Manny and Williams.

A Father's Gift

"Yeah, *boss*. What do you want them to do? Murder me in cold blood?" Manny stared Williams down, narrow eyed. "The trail you're leaving is gettin' easier and easier to follow. It's time for you to rethink your plan. Perhaps we should head back to the sheriff's office and have a conversation." He cocked an eyebrow. "I hear confession is good for the soul."

Hawkins climbed down the steps and joined the group. "Don't be a fool, Manny. You're outnumbered and outgunned. Do as he says." His voice threatened, low and cold.

"Seems to me you're digging yourself a hole, Deputy." Manny glanced back and forth between Williams and Hawkins. "What would you have me believe?" He laughed, the sound short and mirthless. "Let's see if I can imagine how this will play out. We'll find a tree to sit under, palaver. We'll work out an agreement where I accuse you of murder, and you—what? Let me walk away after it's all over? But first you'll apologize for jabbing a pistol in my ribs, for threatening me. Is that how it will go down?"

Williams and Hawkins traded frowns.

"No?" He snorted. "I didn't think so. This cat is out of the bag. We won't return to our lives from five minutes ago. We've burned that bridge. So, I'll say it again. Let's head back to the sheriff's office. Clear the air."

Hawkins stepped closer, with a snarl. Manny almost took a step back but forced himself not to move.

Williams held up a hand. He gestured impatiently at Tommy. "Sit back down." He turned to Manny. "We are all gonna mount our horses." He growled the demand. "We'll take a ride to the country for some fresh air."

Frustration boiled in Manny's chest. *Do not be frightened, and do not be dismayed, for the Lord your God is with you wherever you go.* He straightened. Dug for the anger. Pictured the man in front of him gunning down his dad. Let his rage fuel his courage.

"No."

Hawkins's eyebrows raised in amazement. He placed his hand on the pistol in the holster on his hip. Glared. "Move."

Williams glanced around, a nervous twitch in his eyes. "Dean, don't be so obvious. Folks are looking."

A crack in the dam. Manny let out a breath he wasn't aware he'd held.

A man pushed on the batwing doors in front of the saloon, preparing to leave. He glanced toward the end of the sidewalk but stepped back inside and disappeared when he saw the tense group gathered there.

Manny shook his head. "It appears we're at a Mexican standoff. I'm not going with you. Seems like a foolhardy thing for me to do. And only an idiot would gun me down in the middle of Commerce Street. I don't take you for an idiot, Williams. So where does that leave us?"

"Where, indeed?" A new voice joined the tense party. Manny startled. Williams's eyes widened as he looked over Manny's shoulder at the speaker, who approached. "I 'spect we've reached the part where you both stand down."

Manny frowned. The voice was familiar. The tone was new. Confident and steady.

Williams's face tensed, infuriated. "I told you never to come back here." The words came out in a rushed hiss.

Gabe stepped beside Manny and lined up, shoulder to shoulder. "So you did. I decided not to listen."

Manny risked a glance at Gabe, then his gaze darted back to the men in front of him. The cowhands looked less and less certain they wanted to be here as the seconds dragged on. Hawkins's face flushed red with anger.

"Gabe, what're you doin' here?" Manny spoke out of the side of his mouth.

Hawkins laughed, an ugly sound. "'Gabe?' That's what you're calling yourself now? How sweet. Didn't know you had such soft feelings for that bean eater."

The sheriff slashed the air with his hand. "Hawkins, shut yer trap."

Manny stared at the two men, flummoxed by their reactions. The pieces of the puzzle didn't fit. How did they know Gabe? Why did he choose to put himself in harm's way like this?

Williams waved his pistol. "Stakes are higher this time around, old fool. I won't make the same mistake twice." He spat the words.

Gabe nodded calmly. "Yep. Stakes are definitely higher. Time has a way of making things more dear. The cost I paid was far more than I realized." He shifted, steadied himself. "I decided I'm not paying your ransom any longer. You can't take away any more from me than you already have. But if you're really gonna do it this time, you'll need the stones to pull your trigger in front of all these people." He tipped his head toward the street.

Manny's heart pounded. *What are they talking about?*

Williams took a quick glance over his shoulder. Two men stood near the hitching post, curiosity avid on their faces as they watched. He breathed a curse. He turned to the two cowboys. "Get the horses." He turned to Tommy. "Head back to the ranch."

The men did as they were told. Hawkins watched them leave. Alarm spread across his face. "What're you doin', Rusty? We can't—"

"Shut up and let me think." Williams slashed his hand like a knife.

Hawkins protested. "This'll ruin everything." He gestured toward Manny and Gabe. "We can't just let them walk away."

"Shut up!"

Manny slid his gaze toward Gabe. "What now?" The whisper made it no farther than Gabe's ears.

"Hold your horses." Gabe's answer was just as low.

"Gentlemen." A hearty voice joined the fray. "What's going on?"

Hawkins turned. The false smile Manny had seen before turned his mouth up at the corners. "Boss." He cut his eyes toward Williams. "Just having a chat with some old friends."

Sheriff Moore cocked an eyebrow. "Well, that's mighty strange. Two fellas just rushed to find me. Told me it seemed like a young man was bein' held against his will. Right here in this location." He looked at Williams. "By the old sheriff, of all people. Are you holding this fine citizen against his will?"

Hawkins spluttered. Williams glared.

"I found that curious," Sheriff Moore continued, "so I decided I'd better come check on things. Someone want to tell me what's going on?"

Gabe took a breath. "Sheriff, I think if you do some digging, you'll find several people who can corroborate this story."

Williams made a noise similar to a growl. He stepped toward Gabe but froze when Sheriff Moore leaned in.

Gabe pointed a finger at Rusty. "This man shot and killed an innocent man in cold blood twenty-one years ago."

Williams tripped over a denial.

Gabe ignored him. "I know because I was there. I saw it happen. And I didn't turn him in because he told me he'd kill my boy if I did. He told me to disappear." He turned his sorrowful eyes to Manny. "So, I did. I took off in the opposite direction. Williams came back to San Antonio and got himself hired as the sheriff, pretty much sealing his crime behind an impenetrable wall."

Manny's heart pounded. *Gabe was there?* Carla said his father had been with Luis on the cattle drive. *Did Gabe know my dad?*

Gabe tilted his head toward Hawkins. "And this one was there, too. He's been covering up for Williams ever since. Did you know you work with a criminal, Sheriff Moore? A murderer?"

Hawkins denied it, his words loud with bluster.

Gabe cocked an eyebrow. "Don't you ever get tired of the lies, Dean? Y'all had a long run, but it's over."

Old Sheriff Williams trained his pistol on Gabe. "Mark, I told you to stay away. If it's over for me, it's over for you too."

Manny froze. *Mark?* He stared at Gabe. *Mark? As in, Mark Blair?*

The world around Manny disappeared. The sounds of carriages rattling by on the road behind them, the smell of the bakery down the street, the cold on his face and hands from the December winds. *You're my father?*

A montage of scenes clicked through his mind. Gabe eager to offer his help to a stranger. Gabe content to sleep in the barn with no pay. His knowledge about the tools in the tack room, a room he had built and stocked. His hesitancy to see anyone who would recognize him.

He was tall like Manny. Rubbed his chin when thinking, like Manny. He was sad about missing a loved one, like Manny.

Oh my God.

A memory of pushing a wooden roadrunner toy flashed before his eyes. Mark Blair—no, Gabe—made that toy for him when he was a toddler. The same type of toy he was whittling now for his grandson.

"You've been alive all this time?" Overwhelming hurt arose as Manny stared at the man beside him. Forgotten was the threat of danger. The men, the sheriff. Everything faded. "I don't understand."

Gabe kept his gaze on the tableau unfolding before them. "I can explain."

The unmistakable click of a hammer being cocked pulled Manny's attention back to his surroundings. He flicked his gaze from Hawkins to Williams. Who was preparing to shoot? Who had murder in his heart?

Sheriff Moore took a step forward. "Williams, put your weapon down."

Dean drew a deep breath. "I'm think I'm done lying for you, Rusty."

Williams pointed his gun at the deputy. "Dean, shut your mouth."

Everything happened at once.

Williams pulled his trigger. Sheriff Moore dove to the left, shooting as he rolled. Dean pointed his weapon at his former partner. Manny tackled Williams. The retired sheriff pulled the trigger as he fell. Gabe cried out.

Blood spilled into the dust, soaking quickly into the dirt road. Manny twisted his body away from Williams's, glancing down at himself. No blood. No pain. Where did it come from?

"Gabe, are you all right?" He climbed to his knees. Gabe held a hand against his shoulder where red seeped into his shirtsleeve. A groan pulled Manny's attention away.

Williams lay on his back, clutching his side, his life spilling between his fingers. Sheriff Moore barked orders to bystanders. "Go fetch the doc. Hurry!"

Hawkins slumped against the wall of the building, his hand lax at his side, the pistol lying in the dirt beside him.

He stared at his old partner, eyes wide with amazement. "You shot me."

Sheriff Moore kneeled, pressing his hand against the wound on his chest. "Hold on, Dean. Doc is on his way."

Hawkins coughed weakly. "Knew my past was gonna catch up with me at some point. Shoulda never covered for him." He gasped for breath.

The sheriff glanced at Williams, then looked back at the dying man. "What are you saying, Dean?"

Williams stared at the sky, gritted his teeth. He panted for breath. "Keep your trap shut." He growled the words, defiant despite his pain.

Hawkins shook his head. "Not lying for you anymore." He met Sheriff Moore's gaze. "He killed him. Shot him right in the face. Said no Mexican was gonna ruin his family tree."

"Killed who, Dean?" The sheriff pressed for details.

Dean seemed too spent to answer. Manny jumped in. "If what Carla Williams told me is true, he killed her fiancé, Luis Galindo."

Sheriff Moore looked at Williams. "That true, Sheriff? Did you murder a man?"

Williams laughed, defiant. He coughed blood. His face screwed up in a snarl. "I've killed more men than I can count. And every one of 'em deserved it. I don't know who you're talkin' about." He closed his eyes in denial, belligerence ringing in his tone.

Manny turned to Gabe. "Carla also thought her brother killed my father." He raised his eyebrows in question. "Gabe, was she was wrong about that?"

Gabe sat on the edge of the wooden sidewalk, peered under the palm he had pressed to his shoulder. He looked up. He sighed. Sorrow floated on the air.

"I'm sorry I wasn't there for you, Son."

Chapter Thirteen

Fear clouded Abby's mind like a fog. The due date for the baby was weeks away. No one was at the farmhouse with her. She couldn't do this alone.

"This can't be happening." She muttered while she struggled to the house to change her clothes. "Manny, where are you? You said you'd be back for dinner."

Sham trotted along beside her, his ears perked, eyes tracking her movements.

"Looks like you're gonna be my midwife, boy." Abby patted him, taking comfort in the presence of another soul.

In her bedroom, she peeled away damp clothing, draping the articles over a chair. She stood in the middle of the room, gazing down at her enormous girth. "I can't believe you're going to be here soon. A real person. Someone I've never met." She placed her fingertips against a lump where a tiny limb stretched the muscle of her womb. "Will I love you the moment I first see you? Or will it take a while? I don't even know what you look like."

She stroked her hands in circles on her skin. "We've been waiting on you for the past eight months. Counting the days. Now I'm not so certain. I think we can put this off a while longer. How 'bout it? Let's just stop and think for a moment."

She gasped when the pain struck again. She gritted her teeth. "Wait! I'm not ready." She bent over at the waist.

"Yaideli said to breathe." Abby forced the words between a clenched jaw. Using her nose, she drew in a deep breath, then blew it out through pursed lips. Breathe in. Breathe out. Repeat.

The fist gripping her insides eased up.

"OK, that wasn't so bad." Laughing nervously, Abby straightened. She looked at Sham, who swept the floor with his tail while he sat, watching. "We can do this. I just need to remember what Yaideli told me."

She walked to the trunk at the end of the bed. "First things first. I can't walk around naked. I assume the men in this family are going to remember there is a pregnant woman at home, alone, at some point in the day. They'd be mighty surprised to waltz in and see me in all my glory." Her laugh was shaky. Sham barked.

Abby pulled a nightgown over her head, smoothing it past her belly.

"What else did Yaideli say? We need linens to wrap the baby in. A knife to cut the cord. Cloths to lay under me and for cleaning up after. Oh." She started. "I need to start the fire in the oven so I can boil water."

She poked the embers, then added kindling. In a few moments, flames crackled merrily. She went to the pail in the corner. Almost empty.

Abby sighed. "Come on, boy. We've got to get some water from the well." She pulled on her coat, then bent at the waist when another cramp hit. "Breathe. Just breathe."

When it passed, Abby grabbed the pail by the handle. "Let's get out there and fill this up before the next one comes. I don't know how long this baby is gonna wait. We need to be ready."

After slipping her feet into her boots, she clomped to the well. She lowered the bucket with a splash. The rope tightened when the pail filled with water. The sky above her remained gray and cloudy. The wind carried a sharp bite. Her nose ran. She shivered, her nightgown and coat lending little of the comfort she craved.

Abby cranked the handle heavily, pulling the container to the surface. She turned to wrap the rope around the anchor peg when another contraction struck. She bent, grimacing at the pain. The line slipped through her fingers, and the bucket dropped back to the bottom of the well, landing with a splash.

Abby groaned. The breathing wasn't helping. The pain wouldn't diminish. Would it ease if she straightened? She walked in a circle. The movement seemed to lessen the grip of the cramp. She continued striding around the well, taking small, careful steps. When the discomfort lessened, she drew a deep breath of relief. Pushing a stray wisp of hair from her face, she reached out and cranked the handle again, moving quickly this time.

Once the rope was secured, she pulled the bucket toward her. She tilted it against the kitchen pail and poured until it was full. Turning, she trudged back to the house. She got the kettle on the stove filled before the next pain assailed her.

Abby looked around the empty room. Would it just be this, over and over, until it wore her down? No other chores remained to keep her mind from her fear.

"Manny, where are you?" she cried out. Sham whined. The December wind whistled in the chimney. She was alone.

"God, I need you."

The road to the farm stretched ahead, the Texas winter sun slanting long across the blond fields as it broke through scudding clouds. Details Manny had never noticed seemed gilded by luminescence. Fine lines of black outlined the pine trees. Rays of sun pierced through low-lying clouds in bright, wide beams. A mockingbird trilled from a live oak tree. He was alive. Gabe was alive. Blood coursed through his veins with a tangible pulse. *Thank you, God. My ever-present help.*

A strained silence stretched between Manny and Gabe. After all the words spent in the sheriff's office explaining what had happened, coming up with something to say seemed impossible. How does one respond when one's world is turned upside down in the space of moments?

Manny glanced at the arm Gabe cradled against his chest, the white of a sling standing in stark contrast to his dark cotton shirt.

"Does your arm feel OK?" *He just got shot. How do you think it feels?* Manny swallowed nerves that swamped him now that it was just the two of them.

Gabe quirked a smile in his direction. "I've felt better. But I'll live."

The only sound was the clop of horses' hooves. They walked to lessen the jostling of Gabe's arm.

"I sure didn't intend to be gone this long. Abby's gonna tan our hides. When did you tell her you'd be back?" He looked at the man—his father—riding next to him. "You can't be in more trouble than I am. Dinner has come and gone already."

Gabe coughed. "Actually, I didn't tell her I was leaving."

"Whoa." Manny snorted. "Your tardiness *will* be worse than mine. Good. You can be on the rack instead of me."

The silence resumed. There was so much Manny wanted to ask. Reticence held his tongue.

Gabe sighed. "Manny, I owe you an explanation. And I need to beg forgiveness."

Manny kept his eyes on the road ahead, barely breathing.

"The day Rusty killed Luis, he didn't realize I was there. When he saw me, I thought for sure I was a dead man too. But he slipped his gun back into the holster like he'd just done us all a favor by killing a rattlesnake. He didn't expect me to protest Luis's death."

Gabe shook his head at the memory. "He told me he'd let me live, but I'd have to disappear and never show my face in San Antonio again. Said if I came back, he'd kill you." He looked away. "I should've fought harder for you, but I feared what he might do. I couldn't bear to lose your mother and you both."

Manny snuck a peek at him. Gabe's eyes were glassy. His gaze darted back to the road ahead.

"I did what he said. I roamed the countryside, finding odd jobs here and there. After two years, I couldn't stand it anymore. I decided I was coming home. I'd tell the tale, get him arrested, resume my life. All my courage leaked away when I realized he was the sheriff in town. Who would believe me against him?" The silence stretched again. Gabe's shoulders seemed weighted by shame.

He started to speak. Cleared his throat. Tried again. "Manny, I'm almost certain Rusty started that fire at the barn. He knew I'd returned, had gone against his orders. If he didn't do it himself, he arranged it. It was a message to me. I broke our contract. He was redrawing his line in the sand."

A fist to his belly couldn't have stunned Manny more.

Gabe stopped Buck and faced him head-on. "Son, those scars on your face, everything you endured since then ... it's all my fault. I'm so sorry."

Manny stared, speechless. "G-Gabe, you didn't light that fire. How could you know he'd be so ruthless? I don't blame you for that. Not for a second."

Tension seemed to bleed from Gabe's shoulders. He slumped and took a deep breath.

Wonder lifted a smile to Manny's face. "To know you came back ... you didn't abandon me. You wanted me."

"I missed you every morning of the world." Gabe's voice broke. "When I returned to San Antonio this time, I didn't intend to get involved in your life. It seemed better to let sleeping dogs lie. But when I saw you from the road with that load of wood in the wagon, you looked so much like your mother ... I couldn't stay away. I told myself I'd just talk to you a little, make sure you were OK, then I'd be on my way. It would be enough to know you were happy. I could live with that."

Manny choked back his rejection of that idea.

"When you said Abby would have a baby, I wanted to see her. To lay eyes on the woman who loved my son. I thought *that* would be enough, then I could leave. But I saw the way you both care for each other, how you acted with each other ... I wanted to stay long enough to see the baby."

Gabe shook his head. "I realized I would never be willing to leave. To give up what was stolen from me. And I could see I wasn't the only one suffering. You had something taken from you too." He was silent for a moment. "I had to set things right, even if it meant Rusty killed me. I wanted to replace the picture in your head of who your father was, who he had been. I wanted you to be proud of me."

Manny looked away, unable to maintain eye contact. "Since I was five years old, I've believed you were killed cheating at cards. I accepted that as fact without questioning. I've wronged you."

Gabe's face softened. "You were a child. You can't hold that against yourself." He faced the road, straightening in the saddle. "Besides, we've got a whole new life in front of both of us. Let's let the past lie where it fell and move forward." He grinned. "We need to get a wiggle on. You've got some news to share with Abby."

Chapter Fourteen

Abby paced the floor from bedroom to kitchen and back again. Panic crept from the corners as daylight began to wane. At first, she kept her fear at bay by focusing on annoyance. Manny said he'd be home in plenty of time to eat the noonday meal. Gabe agreed they would cut the door to the bathing room when he returned. Their absence was an inconvenience, nothing more. She'd show them how she didn't need anyone's help when they returned and found everything all lined up, prepared, and waiting for the arrival of her daughter.

But pains came closer now. And lasted longer. They hurt more. An unthinkable thought tried to sneak in.

What if Manny didn't come home? Ever? What if the meeting with that woman had gone south somehow? Manny could be dead.

"Stop it!" She admonished herself. "There is absolutely no reason to think he is dead. You're only scaring yourself."

Except there was a reason to think it. Carla Williams had warned him about the retired sheriff. Gabe tried to talk him out of going. Then Gabe disappeared without telling her.

Panic bubbled in her throat when the next pain struck even quicker than before.

She was going to have this baby alone.

She breathed and walked, consumed by the pains that wouldn't go away.

Another contraction. She leaned forward, gripped the chair back, panting through clenched teeth. Finally, the band squeezing her middle relaxed, and she stood straight. She pointed her face at the ceiling. Tears trickled from the corners of her eyes and leaked into her hair.

"God, I think it's just you and me. I can't worry about what is happening to Manny right now. Help me get my mind set on doing this alone." She dashed her hand fiercely against her eyes, wiping away the dampness.

"What do I need to do?"

She focused on her lessons with Yaideli. When it was time, the pains would be almost nonstop. They weren't quite there yet, but it didn't seem like it would be long. Yaideli's words surfaced in her mind.

"We'll get something for you to pull on when you start pushing. Like a rope, or the leather cinch used on saddles. The traces from the oxen reins. We'll boil them clean, wrap them around the bedposts, and form them into loops at the other end. You'll grab them like your life depends on it and pull. It'll help you focus your energies."

Abby drew a calming breath, nodded to herself.

"When the baby is on its way out, you'll feel an overwhelming urge to push. God made that signal to tell you when to start working hard. You could actually reach down and feel its fuzzy little head if you wanted to. Don't push until then. You'll just wear yourself out."

How close was the baby? Yaideli wasn't here to tell her. She didn't feel the need to push yet, so maybe she still had time.

Boil them clean.

"Oh my. Sham, we've got to get to the barn and gather up some straps. Come with me, boy."

A Father's Gift

Abby slipped her feet into her boots again. She waited for the next contraction. As soon as it eased up, she pulled on her coat, her nightgown billowing out from underneath the hem. She hobbled as quickly as she could manage to the barn, her breath pluming in the cold air.

She pulled the door open and slipped into the warmth of the stable. She hurried to the tack room and unbuckled a cinch strap from one saddle. She was working on the second when the next wave of pain struck.

Gasping, she bent, hands on her knees. She panted through the next sixty seconds, tears squeezing from her eyes.

The urge to push suddenly overwhelmed her.

"No, this can't happen now. Not here." Abby reached down with her fingertips and felt a hard, bony curve where she expected nothing but softness. "No. No."

She could make it back to the house. She took two steps, then stumbled to her knees.

"God, help me."

Voices penetrated the haze of pain. The door pulled open, letting in the dying light of the afternoon. Manny! He was home.

"She'll be shocked—Abby! Abby-girl, what on earth are you doing out here in your nightgown?" Manny's boots thumped to the ground when he hurled himself from the horse. He crouched beside her.

She reached a trembling hand toward him. "The baby. It's coming." The words wheezed between her panting breaths.

"What? Now? It's too soon." He gathered her close.

Abby huffed. "Tell that to the baby."

"Let's get you to the house." He stood, cradling her in his arms and turned.

"No! Put me down. It's coming. It's coming now. I can't wait." Abby tucked her chin to her chest and strained. Her face turned red.

"Whoa, whoa! Abby, stop."

She ignored him, all energy focused inward. The tendons in her neck stood out.

"Gabe! What do we do?" Manny turned helplessly to his father.

Using his good hand, Gabe was already shaking out the blanket he'd been using at night. He tossed it over the pile of hay that acted as his bed and straightened it as well as he could. "Lay her down."

Abby gasped a huge lungful of air and relaxed, the contraction over for the moment. She let her head drop back against Manny's shoulder.

"You can't have the baby in the barn, Abby. You have to stop."

"If it was good enough for Jesus, it's good enough for our child." She bit the words out, eyes closed. "It's not like I have any control over what's happening."

"Lay her down, just long enough to check the progress." Gabe's voice was calm. "I helped your mother when you came. I can tell you what to do."

Manny carried her to the straw bed and laid her gently down. Bird poked her head over the wall between stalls, ears pricked forward as she investigated the strange goings-on.

"Check to see if the baby is crowning."

Manny looked at him, eyes wild. "What?"

Abby huffed a quiet laugh. "Welcome to my world, dear husband." She glanced at Gabe. "If by crowning you mean is the head showing, the answer is yes."

Manny lifted Abby's nightgown. "Criminy, Gabe. He's practically here already. What do we do?"

Gabe chuckled. "We let nature take its course. Shouldn't take long now."

"Take long? It's right now!" Manny's voice sounded panicked.

"You just be ready to catch it when it slips out." Gabe pulled the towel he'd been using for bathing from a nearby nail. "Use this to wrap the babe in."

"Catch it?" The terrified look on Manny's face made Abby snort.

She tucked her chin again and groaned. "Here comes another one."

Manny kneeled in front of her and grasped her hands. "Hold on to me. I'm here."

The contraction pulled her into a curled position, knees pressing against her chest. Her hand squeezed Manny's until his fingers turned white. Gabe slipped in behind her. "I'm gonna help you from here. We're gonna put some pressure on the babe by leaning forward. We'll just help it along."

Abby gritted her teeth and growled. Every muscle in her body strained.

Sham lay flat on the floor, his head resting on his paws, ears flattened. He whined when Abby's groan stretched on.

She gasped for air when the contraction eased, leaning against Gabe like he was her own father. Funny how all of her concerns melted away in the face of the coming child.

Manny glanced up, excited wonder lighting his face. "I think one more good push, and his head will be out, Abby-girl. Give it all you got on this next one."

Abby breathed shallow breaths while she waited. Gabe rubbed her shoulders. She swallowed. "Here it comes."

She tucked in, and Gabe propped her from behind. "Arghhhhh!" Her eyes screwed tight as she strained, every muscle quivering. Manny looked up, fright tensing his face. She couldn't worry about him now. This baby was more important than either of their fears.

"Come on, girl. I can see his ears." Manny sounded as excited as a boy being introduced to his first horse.

Abby pushed like her life depended on it. The pressure released some when the baby's head emerged. "Is she out?" Abby stretched to peer past the hem of her nightgown but could see nothing.

"Just the head." Manny looked up, grinning from ear to ear.

Gabe shifted. "Clear the membranes from the babe's face if they're still there. Open the airways. Next push will be the slippery one, Manny. Be ready to catch him—"

"Her," Abby interrupted. "It's a girl. I know it. And ... arghhh ..."

She used every ounce of strength to push one more time. A gasp of relief escaped her lungs as the baby slid out.

"Got 'im!" Manny held up the baby boy in both hands. The infant wriggled and flailed, gasping past the water in his lungs. The smile on Manny's face lit the entire room. Seconds later, a wail emerged.

Sham lifted his head, ears perked up, head cocked to the side. He barked once. An ox lowed from the front of the barn.

Abby laughed, tears streaming down her face. "I was so sure it was a girl. We really are like the nativity scene. A baby boy born in a stable."

Manny laid the child on the towel. Gabe handed him a knife from his waist. "Go ahead, Papa. Cut the cord." He smiled proudly as he handed it over.

"Wait." Abby held up a hand. "Tie it off first."

Manny cut a rawhide thong from his hat and sliced through it with the knife, cutting off a smaller piece. He

tied two knots onto the cord using the thong, then cut between them.

The baby squalled like he'd been mortally wounded. They all laughed. Every eye in the room was damp. Manny wrapped the slippery body tenderly in the towel and handed him to Abby. She looked into the red, angry face, enthralled.

"Oh, my goodness," she crooned. "So upset with the world." She stroked a fingertip along his eyebrow, mesmerized by his perfection. "I promise, it gets better, little one."

She groaned when another contraction hit. "Again?" She frowned, shifting on the bed of straw.

"It's normal." Gabe spoke up. "Just your body getting rid of the afterbirth. Manny, you can press your hand against her stomach, help push it along."

Manny moved up onto his knees and placed the heel of his hand against her belly. He pressed lightly, then stopped. "Is it supposed to feel this hard?" He looked at Gabe with concern.

Abby groaned louder. "It feels like I need to push again. This isn't what Yaideli said would happen. Is everything OK?"

Manny leaned back to check. "Oh, my stars. Abby, I see another head."

She hardly acknowledged what he said, focused entirely on the message her body sent. Gabe took the baby boy from her arms. Holding him against his side, he propped her from behind.

"All right, little lady. One more time. Looks like you're gonna have two babies at the end of today instead of one." He supported her shoulders. Abby's growl filled the barn for a second time.

As if the first baby had broken new ground, the second one slid out with hardly a whisper of protest. Moments later, Manny held the small body up, tears of joy on his face. "You got your girl, sweet wife. Meet baby number two."

Gabe shrugged the sling off his arm and tossed it over. "Here, use this until we can get everyone into the house."

Abby lay back, exhausted. "That better be all."

Her tired mutter elicited peals of proud, joyful laughter from the men.

Gabe helped her sit up. He slipped the baby boy into her arms. He hugged her tightly, emotion clogging his throat. "I couldn't be prouder of you, Abby. Llamado de la sangre es fuerte. I'm blessed to have you as a daughter-in-law." Manny leaned forward and handed her the infant girl.

Her arms full of babies, Abby frowned. Where had she heard that phrase before. *The call of the blood is strong.* Yaideli. She'd said it at her house the night she left. Awareness loomed at the edge of her consciousness. She looked between the two men, both looking pleased as punch and bursting to tell her something.

"Daughter-in-law?" She gasped. "Oh my." She stared at him. "Gabe. You're his father, aren't you? That's why you came. Why you stayed, even when I was so horrible to you." She looked at Manny, tears flooding her eyes again. "Manny, how wonderful! But I don't understand."

Manny smiled at his father. "We'll tell you all about it, but let's get all of you to the house and cleaned up."

Abby closed her eyes, tears of absolute contentment trickling onto her temples. "Just a second. No one move. I want to remember this moment for the rest of my life."

The warm, earthy smell of the barn filled her nose with familiar comfort. Sham's tail wagged slowly back and forth, swishing through the straw, as steady as the arm of a grandfather clock. Bird blew air through her

nose, stretching her neck as far over the dividing wall as it would go, sniffing the air. The oxen mooed. Bosque and Buck both waited patiently to be turned into their stalls. Manny kneeled at her side, beaming like a newly born star. Gabe—his tired, dear face suddenly more precious to her than almost anything—looked like a man who'd just been given the moon and sun. The babies in her arms mewled like tiny kittens, fingers curled into fists.

"Thank you, Father. I ... I don't even know how to say how blessed I feel. Just, thank you." She smiled at Manny, tears of joy brimming in her eyes. "I know it's a few days early, but I don't think any gift will ever top this one. Merry Christmas."

About the Author

A fifth-generation Texan, **Paula Peckham** graduated from the University of Texas in Arlington and taught math at Burleson High School for nineteen years. She and her husband, John, divide their time between their home in Burleson and their casita in Rio Bravo, Mexico. Her debut novel, Protected, was an ACFW Genesis semi-finalist in 2020. She also writes short stories, novellas, and poems. She had contributions in the 2021 release Christmas Love Through the Ages, and Texas Heirloom Ornament. She is the president of ACFW DFW and is a member of Unleashing the Next Chapter. She has spoken at ACFW, Unleashing the Next Chapter, and the Carrollton League of Writers. For more about Paula and her books, follow her at paulapeckham.com.

Protected by Paula Peckham

Thank You!

I appreciate your purchase of my book. Your support means so much to me. If you enjoyed it, there is one more thing you can do. Please follow the link below and leave a review on Amazon. Not sure what to say? Here are some suggestions.

Start with a hook, a sentence that grabs the potential reader's attention. Something like, "Wow, if you want to stay up all hours of the night reading, this is the book for you!"

List your praise and your critiques. No book is perfect. Potential readers will probably consider it a more realistic review if you share things you didn't love. But be as lavish as you want with what you really liked.

Talk about the characters. When people decide about a new book to buy, they want to know if the people in the story are authentic and realistic, not too perfect to be true.

Discuss whether the dialogue sounded real to you or gave the story a good regional flavor.

Maybe you liked the descriptions of the setting, little details that made the time period pop to life.

Give your recommendation. Who do you think would enjoy reading the book?

Your review doesn't have to be long. A few sentences will suffice. Choose only one of the suggestions listed above, or all. Up to you! Your words may be just the thing to swing a reader into the decision to buy.

The payoff for an author comes from the Amazon algorithm. Once an author collects the magic number of reviews (some say 25, some say 50—it's a mystery), Amazon shows the book in more search results, which means more readers will see it when they shop.

Personally, I want to hear what you have to say. Just know, you taking the time and effort to add a review to Amazon, Goodreads, Barnes & Noble—wherever you like to check out books—will mean the world to the authors you enjoy. We can't do this alone and we appreciate every single one of you.